Protocol
Omega

Roman Kubinski

ISBN: *978-1-0685867-1-2*

CONTENTS

ACKNOWLEDGMENTS

First of all, I would like to sincerely thank everyone who contributed to the creation of this book and were an invaluable support to me throughout the entire creative process.

I am especially grateful to my family, whose unwavering belief in me and my abilities gave me strength in moments of doubt. Your support, and understanding were the foundation upon which I could rely throughout the journey. Without your love and compassion, this project would never have come to life.

Special thanks also go to Joanna Woronowska, whose support and insightful comments were of great importance to me at every stage of the creative process. Her help with proofreading the text and her inspiring presence shaped this book into what it is today. Your belief in this project was a constant source of motivation for me.

I must also acknowledge the creators of the work "The Golden Book" by Saint Germain, whose work and passion had a profound impact on me and what I have been able to create. Their work was not only an inspiration to me but also one of the most important influences in my life.

Thank you to everyone who contributed to the making of this book, both directly and indirectly. Every bit of support, every kind gesture, and every encouraging word meant a great deal and helped bring about what you now hold in your hands.

With heartfelt gratitude,

Roman Kubinski

PROLOGUE

In truth, my name doesn't really matter. I could just as easily be called anything in any language. The same goes for where I was born and where I come from...

I am, however, aware that for you, names and places are important, giving them that unfortunate significance. I know that without these it would be hard for you to navigate my story. Like a ship drifting aimlessly without an anchor in an unknown direction—you need a name, a place, a time, as a reference point for your imagination... That semblance of an anchor to tether the story to the reality you know, the world that will serve as your frame of reference.

You are important to me and because of that, your needs have meaning for me. Let's agree that my name is John, and I come from the United Kingdom. Living in a small town, Burton on Trent, working a rather insignificant job. I am an unremarkable person who marvels at the beauty of the local swans, having walked this beautiful and peculiar planet for over 40 years.

For now, that should be enough to anchor my story in your imagination, your consciousness, your perception of reality...

To begin that wonderful moment from which everything starts, and before you the great unknown unfolds, where nothing is impossible, and after the journey ends, nothing will ever look the same.

I hope you are ready for my story. It would be better if you were ready for what you are about to experience, but if you're not, it won't matter. The greatest changes often come unexpectedly, though on a deeper level, they've long been planned.

So, ready or not, here is my story...

1 ANATEA

I was sitting on the grass admiring the beauty of the surroundings. This time I must have wandered quite far as I didn't recognize the place. Just a beautiful, magnificent meadow, harmoniously filled with lovely flowers. Thankfully, the birds weren't too noisy so I could relax for a moment, captivated by the nature around me. I could almost swear there was a hidden melody within the mysterious symphony of sounds, expressing an irresistible melancholy yet also a mysterious beauty. Oddly, I couldn't see the river that I usually walked along. I must have, in deep thought, strayed from the familiar paths and stumbled upon this extraordinary place.

"Hi."

I heard a voice, faintly, at the edge of my awareness. A word that pulled me out of my deep reverie and contemplation of the nature surrounding me.

"Hi."

I heard again, the clear voice of a young girl, as if coming from behind me.

"My name is Anatea. What's yours? You must have come from far away, since we haven't met before. You don't look like my friends from around here."

"Hi," I replied in an irritated tone, as the sense of awe I had felt for the nature around me suddenly vanished as mysteriously as it had filled me earlier.

"What's your name?" she asked again.

"John," I answered shortly, my voice still tinged with irritation. "Just John."

"That's kind of strange..." the girl said. "You must be from far away."

"John is a strange name to you? It's one of the most common names around here. Anatea is the strange name if you ask me. I'd say you're the one who must've come from a far-off place," I replied dryly. "Unless you made it up for fun, or maybe that's just what your friends call you?"

"No, it's my name," she said, surprised. "Why would I make up a name? After all, it expresses who we are."

Those words sounded odd coming from a child. They didn't fit the maturity of her youthful voice.

I turned around and looked at her. She seemed about 10 years old. She was wearing a dress with incredible colours. A smiling child with blonde hair and delicate skin, but something calm and deep shone in her blue eyes. I had the strange feeling I was looking at someone much older and more mature than her small childlike frame suggested. I even felt she was more mature than me. I'd risk saying that an elderly woman was looking at me through the eyes of a young child.

Instinctively, I sensed something was definitely off about what I was seeing, and this feeling caused a strange unease to stir in my stomach.

"John sounds wise. You're probably an advisor or a 'knowing one.' Are you here to expand your knowledge? Where do you come from?"

Her words sounded even stranger than the impression she gave me. And what on earth is a "knowing one"?

"Burton," I replied, increasingly torn by my emotions. On one hand I was standing in front of a little girl, but on the other hand, I couldn't shake the feeling that I was the child in her presence.

"I'm from Burton. Burton-on-Trent," I repeated in an uncertain voice, trying to suppress the strange feeling that was steadily growing inside me.

"Burton? I've never heard of such a place. It must be far away."

"Not that far. I couldn't have walked too far. I usually go on a few-kilometre walks; a few times I ventured over ten kilometres from home. For longer distances, I take my bike or motorbike. I love motorcycles—they give such an unrestrained sense of freedom."

"I've spent my whole life here. My parents don't let me wander far. They think I'm too young for adventures, but I don't think so. One day I'll travel the whole world, all the worlds—no universe will hold any secrets from me. What's a motorbike?" she asked suddenly, completely catching me off guard.

"What do you mean, 'What's a motorbike?' You've never seen one?"

"I don't know. How can I say whether I've seen a motorbike or not when I don't even know what it is?"

At that moment, I froze, stunned by a sudden realization. Though I had clearly heard her words, she hadn't moved her lips once. How could I hear her if she wasn't actually saying anything? I realized that I hadn't heard her words at all—her thoughts had turned into sounds in my mind.

That's impossible. She's just a child. This must be a dream. I must have fallen asleep in the meadow, and this is just an ordinary dream. I need to wake up, but it was already too late.

Terror, wild terror, began to fill me. An emotion that felt so out of place in this peaceful setting. I couldn't wake up, but I couldn't stay here either. I had to run, run far away from this child who wasn't a child. Run as far as possible. Return home and forget. Forget and suppress this as if it had never happened.

I started to run, fleeing from the terrifying child. I ran faster and faster, trying to find my way back. Running, trying to remember how I got here. So that, in the safety of my home, I could just forget. I ran faster and faster, struggling to catch my breath.

Struggling not to lose my sanity after what I had experienced, but I couldn't forget, I couldn't. What had happened was too deeply etched into my memory. I wouldn't be able to bear it. I wouldn't be able to bear these feelings, these thoughts. Sleep or wake, anything, just to escape from here... My vision began to blacken. I lost consciousness...

Blissful unawareness...

2 KASELIN

I woke up suddenly in my bed. That was a really, really strange dream. Everything felt so realistic, and I can recall every detail as if it had actually happened.

It wasn't one of those nightmares where you wake up drenched in sweat, screaming, but which quickly fades from memory, leaving only a vague feeling of unease that eventually disappears. I remember this dream in vivid detail, as if it were a memory of yesterday, still fresh in my mind. And then there was that child... I could feel their presence so clearly. Thankfully, the warmth of my bed calmed my thoughts and emotions. Whatever it was, it didn't matter anymore. Now, I was lying safely in my bed, and that was all that counted. Warmth and safety—those were the only important things now.

Despite the comfort of my bed, my thoughts wouldn't stop. They ran like unleashed dogs, sprinting ahead uncontrollably, ignoring any attempt to call them back. They wouldn't slow down for even a second, just racing forward at a frantic pace...

But was it really a child? It's impossible for such a delicate figure to carry such an odd depth. And what they said—or rather, how they said it. No, wait, they didn't speak.

They placed thoughts directly into my mind. Thank God it's all over now. It was just a bad dream, like any other, and now I'm finally home, safe...

I need to shake off these memories, wake up properly. Coffee, a good coffee with milk and a teaspoon of sugar, enjoyed in my garden, should bring me back to life. The cool, refreshing morning air should help too. Yes, coffee— that's what I need to make all these bad memories fade.

Alright, I've got a plan. Get up from bed, head to the kitchen, make a good, delicious cup of coffee, sit in the garden, take in the view, and start a fresh new day. The rest will follow as it always does... What day is it, anyway? I couldn't remember. Strange—I always know what day it is. My internal clock always worked perfectly, but now nothing. It was as if time had stopped. It could be Monday or Saturday for all I knew. I jumped out of bed. What if I need to be at work soon and I'm still here, stuck in bed, thinking about stupid dreams! I need to get moving fast because if I'm late again, I'll have much bigger problems than some idiotic dream. Unless it's Saturday or Sunday— then I'm saved. Change of plan. First, check what day it is, and then either get to work or follow the original plan.

Knock, knock.

Starting the day with neighbours banging next door—just great. They're really lovely people, but making a racket with renovations while I'm still asleep is too much. It's one thing to tolerate noise during the day—everyone makes changes in their homes from time to time—but so early in the morning? That's too much. I'll need to have a word with them later. I have to remember they're nice elderly people who sometimes collect packages for me and resist the urge to go off on them. Note to self—old people, be polite.

Sometimes it's hard to smile when everything is boiling inside, but I'm a good neighbour, and I won't show them my superiority. I'll be kind because that's what good manners dictate, and I'm a very well-mannered person. Kind and polite—I thought of myself with satisfaction and a sense of superiority over those ordinary elderly folks.

Knock, knock, knock.

The new knocking interrupted my thoughts of how magnanimously I'd handle the neighbours instead of showing them how they'd overstepped...

Suddenly, I realized the knocking wasn't coming from next door—it was at my door. Someone was knocking on my bedroom door! Someone's lost their mind. They're in my house, knocking on my door? My bedroom door??? What the hell!

Whoever you are, you have no idea what trouble you've gotten yourself into... I'm going to tear you to pieces!!!

I've never jumped out of bed so fast. I almost ran to the door, filled with fury, ready to crush whoever was behind it. In my mind, I already saw my opponent, taking them down with quick blows, triumphing over the unlucky fool who'd chosen the wrong house to burgle.

I threw the door open with force and froze. Standing before me was a short, slender woman, around 160 cm tall, elderly, who said with amusement in her voice:

"A burglar knocking on doors—that would certainly be high-class robbery. Should I perhaps ask if I may burgle you, good sir? Such politeness would surely impress you. By the way, I don't mean to be rude, but opening the door to an elderly woman while completely naked isn't exactly polite, wouldn't you say, young man? Don't you think it would be better to tear someone to pieces while at least somewhat dressed? Doing it completely naked, well, that would be rather barbaric, wouldn't you agree?"

I was dumbfounded. Indeed, I sleep naked, and in my rush of emotions, I'd completely forgotten about it. Now I felt like a little boy, quickly trying to cover myself.

"My name is Kaselin..."

"John," I replied in a voice so unnatural I barely recognized myself. I stood there rooted to the spot, watching what was happening, but what exactly was happening? I couldn't wrap my head around it.

In my own home, an older woman—she must've been over fifty—stood before me, laughing at me when she should be terrified that I caught her. What in the world is going on? This is too much, even for me, and believe me, I've seen a lot in my life.

"What do you think you're doing? I'm calling the police, or better yet, I'll handle this myself!"

"Perhaps you'd like to take a sip of coffee first? It's just how you like it—with milk and one teaspoon of sugar. And don't worry about the police; we don't have any, so no one will be coming. With a disarming smile, the woman replied, 'I'm here to help you, not to harm you. You're in much deeper trouble than you realize.'"

"Help me? You must be joking. You'll be the one needing help soon, and I mean medical help."

"I think a sip of delicious coffee will help you, and we can talk calmly," she replied calmly, unbothered by my words or the tone of my voice. "Besides, hospitals aren't needed here either."

"What do you mean, no police or hospitals? I don't live in the middle of the jungle; this is Burton. It may not be a big city, but come on..."

"Have some coffee and let's sit down and talk. I'm responsible for visitors like you who have trouble finding their way here. I provide assistance and explain things, but I must admit, I've never encountered a case like yours.

18

Honestly, I don't think anyone has dealt with something quite like your situation before."

"Whatever your job is, that's really none of my business. But the fact that you're uninvited in my home most certainly is, and believe me you won't get away with this. Who the hell are you?"

"I already told you—Kaselin, and you know what I do."

"Kaselin? Is that your last name? Can't you just tell me your first name?"

"Kaselin is my first name. I trust you can accept that."

"Alright, so what are you doing in my house, Kaselin?"

"I think we should start by clarifying where we really are, as that seems to be the first thing we need to sort out."

"What do you mean, where we are?!" I nearly shouted, trying to gather my thoughts while grappling with the absurdity of what she was saying. "You're an intruder in my home—that's where we are!"

"Look out the window," she replied calmly. "Looking outside your box can drastically change your perspective on things."

"What is she talking about?" I thought, but her voice somehow didn't allow for resistance. Without thinking, I walked over to the window and looked outside. What I saw was beyond anything I expected. I froze.

"Welcome to Earth," she said.

"And where else would we be if not on Earth?!" I shouted hysterically.

"Perhaps now you'll have some coffee, and we can talk calmly?" she said with remarkable composure. "I understand how difficult this must be for you—it's quite a surprise for us too..."

3 EARTH

For a long moment I slowly sipped my coffee, staring at the woman across from me. She looked like a petite woman with light hair and blue eyes, but it was clear she was in excellent physical shape, and there was an inner dignity radiating from her that I couldn't quite wrap my head around. The long silence allowed me to calm down a bit and collect my emotions. "Welcome to Earth"? Where the hell else should we be? This wasn't Earth; this was some kind of damn science fiction. What I saw outside the window would shame even the most extravagant visions of the future from the greatest creators of our time. How was it possible that my small, cramped apartment in Burton was at the very centre of an unimaginable futuristic city?

"Maybe because it's not your apartment," she replied in her typically calm manner. "We created it based on your memories so you'd feel safe in a familiar environment," she said, as if reading my thoughts. "We don't know why you're here, but the fact that we don't know doesn't mean anything yet. A lack of awareness of a cause doesn't exclude its existence."

"What do you mean, you created this place based on my memories?" I couldn't shake the thought. The very fact that they could, as she claimed, access my memories was already terrifying, but the thought of what else they might find was even worse...

"We analysed your memories and recreated your room as faithfully as possible based on them. I hope we succeeded well enough for you to feel at home here."

"You messed with my mind?!"

"We really want to help you," she said.

"And I'm supposed to just take your word for it?"

"Our understanding of the soul and body is very different from your way of thinking. We know you don't believe in God or other beings, but just because you don't believe in something doesn't mean it doesn't exist. In your past, people believed the Earth was flat, but did that mean it truly was?"

"Well, okay, the way ancient people thought reflected their level of advancement—they didn't have the means to see how things really looked like we can now."

"I couldn't have said it better, but as you can see, the reality surrounding you is not the familiar reality of the 21st century, so our understanding reflects the times we live in."

"Well, that makes a lot of sense. So, what is your way of perceiving reality?" I asked, genuinely intrigued by what she was saying. Maybe by accident, she'd reveal some great secret of the universe that would make me famous when I returned—a secret that was as obvious to her as the fact that the Earth is a sphere drifting through the vastness of the solar system.

"Our way of perceiving reality is literally the opposite of what you're used to. You believe that the brain and its neural impulses create consciousness. We know it's exactly the other way around. The soul expresses its essence in this reality through the filter called the brain. Imagine that the human body is a car, and the driver is the soul. It would be foolish to think that the car creates the driver. It's the driver who, through their decisions, steers the car. They may choose a fast sports car that provides unforgettable experiences or a powerful truck capable of doing heavy work. You select a car based on the job you plan to do. In the same way, the soul chooses the body that will be most helpful for the path it has planned. A car without a driver wouldn't be able to accomplish anything.

Let me give another example: just as a TV cannot generate an image on its own and needs omnipresent waves broadcast by a TV station, so too the brain cannot express anything without the soul that manifests through it."

"What does that have to do with my memories?"

"Going back to the car analogy, don't your cars have cameras that can document situations in case of an unfortunate event?"

"So what? What's your point?"

"Your memories are recorded for the needs of the soul, like a computer file that contains everything that has happened in your life. And as you know, computer files can be freely copied and their contents used on another computer."

"So, I'm just a data file to you? Is this all one big simulation?"

"No, John, this is reality. Your Earth is as real as this one. This is just an attempt to explain our way of thinking and how we've managed to do what we've done."

"Go on."

"In the same way, the memories of one life can be copied by other souls to expand their experience. Have you ever wondered why so many people under hypnosis remember being Cleopatra? Do you really believe there were that many Cleopatra's in the world? Her life was simply such a valuable lesson that it was copied by other souls to enrich their own experiences and learn from it."

"So, you copied my memories like they were just some ordinary computer file? That's a blatant violation of privacy!"

"It was necessary to help you, I had to understand who you are and how you perceive reality. This was the most efficient way. As for privacy, it's just an illusion—much like how a flat Earth was an illusion to ancient people. Do you really believe you can keep any privacy before God?"

"God doesn't exist."

"That's your perspective, not ours."

"And what is yours?"

"I'm not saying I'm God, far from it, but privacy is only an illusion that ceases to exist on higher levels. However, don't worry—beings that exist on such a high level that privacy no longer exists will still respect it because they understand that it's important to you. Knowing your perspective on reality allows me to help you more effectively."

"So you know my life as if you've lived it yourself?" I asked, horrified because it certainly wasn't the life of the most wonderful human being to walk the Earth.

"How else would I know what a car is?"

"Or a motorcycle..." I mused for a moment.

"Yes, everything you know, I know, and even more because your memory gaps are almost terrifying. It must be so hard for you to function, remembering so little."

"Sometimes it can be a blessing. My life wasn't easy."

"I agree. You've experienced a lot of suffering."

"But what about the fact that you don't have cars?" I couldn't wrap my head around it. I couldn't imagine a world without cars.

"Probably as people once couldn't imagine a world without horses. They literally formed the foundation of civilization."

"Yeah, it's hard to imagine life in ancient times without them."

"Fortunately, there are more efficient ways to travel than moving on the ground. Roads would only destroy the beauty of the surrounding nature. After all, this is the Great Genetic Library of Life. Roads would desecrate it by their mere presence."

"The Great Library? Is that where we are now? I've never heard that term before."

"You could say that. Mother Earth—the whole planet—is the great library of this galaxy. It is also the home and child of Lord Romasz."

The whole planet? I couldn't wrap my head around it— how could an entire planet be a library? That's the only thing I focused on now. The very idea fascinated me. Mother Earth... I wondered if they used that term customarily or if it held deeper significance for them.

"Let's move forward in small steps, but I promise that in time I'll answer all your questions. For now know that you are surrounded by friends, and we want to help you. The rest will become clear in time... The coffee has probably gone cold by now. Rest a bit, and I'll prepare you a meal. You've had too many new experiences for now. You need time to calm down, gather your thoughts, and ground yourself in this new reality, which is so different from everything you've known."

There was compassion and warmth in her eyes, which somehow calmed me. I trusted her. I didn't know her, but I felt I could fully trust her in everything.

With that, she left my bedroom, leaving me alone. I walked to the window and looked out. Words cannot describe what I saw through it. It was like taking someone from ancient times and placing them in the middle of London. I was on what must have been the hundredth floor, surrounded by other monumental buildings, yet there was plenty of space between them. Each building was designed to seamlessly blend into the panorama of this metropolis. I could say that there were various flying ships, from small to massive ones, but is a car really just a modern-day chariot? Sort of, but not entirely.

The gap between an ancient person and modern-day London is nothing compared to the gap between me and what I was now looking at. Is that an accurate description? I can't say. I can't even understand the purpose of most of the objects surrounding me. One thing is certain: what I am experiencing now will change.

4 BREAKFAST

I looked around my room. The meticulous attention to detail with which it was recreated was beyond my understanding. Even the bed linen was slightly stale, just like mine, because I never washed it often enough. In the corner of the bedroom, under the ceiling, was the familiar cobweb that I had been planning to remove for weeks. I approached the bookshelf, and even the books were slightly dusty, with visible signs of use. I opened my favourite book, and to my surprise, it was filled with notes I had written by hand. I didn't remember most of them, yet they were clearly in my handwriting.

It's incredible how precisely the details of our lives are recorded—so detailed that it's hard to comprehend. On one hand, it's fascinating that such small details are important enough to be documented in the story of my life. But at the same time, I felt uneasy knowing that everything I had done could be available to other beings. And trust me, not everything in my life is worthy of praise or remembrance. I'm just a regular person walking through life, not always making the right choices. I'm not exactly proud of everything, and some things I'd prefer to forget with all my heart.

"Breakfast," I heard from beyond the wall. "It's served, please come before it gets cold."

I instinctively moved to the next room. The pleasant smell filled the space. I must admit I was a bit apprehensive about what they ate here. It could have been a simple pill that fulfill led all my body's nutritional needs. Who knows what might have crossed their minds after all this time?

To my great surprise, there was a large portion of a traditional English breakfast on the table—but not just any English breakfast, the best one I'd ever had in my life. It was from that restaurant on the 46th floor when I was on a trip to London. How could she know this was my favourite?

Right, I think I know. She knew everything about me that I knew about myself. And who knows, maybe even more. The thought chilled me.

"Don't worry, I don't judge you negatively in any way. This is all part of your growth process. You're still very, very young. You have every right to make mistakes. These mistakes aren't something to be ashamed of but should be treated as friends helping you grow, develop, and gain experience. After all, that's why you were born—to grow, and only those who do nothing make no mistakes."

"Could you please get out of my head?" I said in an irritated tone. I couldn't have even a moment of privacy, couldn't reflect calmly on what had happened to me without being overheard. "You know, where I come from, privacy is a highly valued and respected aspect of life. You can't just disregard it because you have different views. So I ask you to give me a bit of privacy, at least in my thoughts."

"I am your friend, and I'm here to help you. Understanding you is crucial to this process. Of course, I'll respect your request if that's your wish, but from my perspective, truly knowing you is very important. How can I take wise action or fully understand you if I don't know what's happening?"

"I think you already know far too much about me, and I'd greatly appreciate it if you honoured my request."

"As you wish. Free will is sacred, and as I've said, I'll respect your request. I also enjoy challenges, and this will be something completely new for me."

"I'm not that young anymore. After all, I'm in my forties now. Who knows, I might have passed the halfway point of my life, and it's all downhill from here. Honestly, you're not that much older than me, and considering you're a woman, in my eyes, you'll always be a young, beautiful woman. Maybe not 18, since you have quite a bit of experience. Let's agree on 21? How about that?"

"That's very kind of you, but I didn't mean the age of your body. I was talking about the age of your soul. Even telepathy is still beyond your reach, and that's the basic form of communication in the universe. Compared to your life, it's as if you were a few months old, just learning to walk and make decisions, experiencing their effects first-hand. I'm not saying this to offend you, but to make you understand that from my perspective, you're still very, very young. You have the right to make mistakes that, when you're older, won't happen anymore. Someone who already knows how to run doesn't make the mistakes of someone who's just learning to walk."

Remember, I'm your friend, here to help you, not judge. I truly understand how extraordinary and perhaps frightening this all is for you."

"How can I be sure that you truly want to help me, and I'm not just some zoo animal that you'll show off as a relic from the past?"

"I'm not sure if you are a relic of the past, as there was no moment in our history that matches your memories. But the universal law of unity compels us to do everything in our power to help you in your situation."

"The law of unity? Are you saying that all people, as representatives of one council, are obligated to help each other?"

"In a sense, you're right, but that's a vast simplification, which I can explain further if you wish. But for now, please eat, you wouldn't want everything to get cold, would you?"

Indeed, everything smelled so divine that it would be a shame for it to lose even a bit of its wonderful flavour just because I was talking too much. That would be an unforgivable sin, I thought with a laugh. I hadn't even realized how hungry I was, and the craftsmanship with which this was prepared made it so that even if I wasn't hungry, I would still eat everything on my plate out of sheer gluttony. You don't turn down a feast like this.

"I hope you like it. I tried to prepare it the best I could."

It'll be hard to get used to this openness, and her wonderful, radiant smile left no doubt that she had heard my thoughts.

"Privacy," I said with a slight irritation in my voice.

"I'll make the necessary adjustments after breakfast, you have my word."

"Thank you, that's very kind of you."

"I'll do anything to help you, and if it's important to you, then of course I'll respect it."

The food tasted truly exquisite—far better than what I had in London. Any alteration to this perfect dish would have been ruining its flawless perfection.

"You're probably the best cook in the world," I said, my voice filled with awe.

"Thank you. In fact, it wasn't that difficult. I didn't prepare this meal in the way you're familiar with."

"Do you have robots that cook for you? That must be an amazing convenience. No dirty dishes, no grocery shopping—just pure joy in savouring the dishes served. I could get used to that."

"There's actually a much simpler solution. As you know, matter, at its core, is just a manifestation of energy. There are infinite amounts of energy all around us, and all you need is the ability to access it.

With my will, I can influence this energy and shape it into any form, such as a delicious meal. In reality, anything is possible."

"That's amazing, so at any moment, I could create a perfectly chilled beer and enjoy its taste?"

"Only as long as you could focus your will to achieve the desired effect. After a few rounds, that would be difficult to do."

"If it's so simple, why can't I do it? I wouldn't need to go to work, or grocery shopping, no more hunger or wars over resources. Life would be so much easier."

"That's an excellent question. As a human, it's your innate ability, just like telepathy and other natural abilities, which for some reason, you currently lack. It's just another mystery on a rather long list."

I ignored her remark. I had enough chaos in my head already, and the last thing I wanted was to add more to the confusion that had replaced my usually focused mind.

31

Just yesterday, I was in my city, living my life with ordinary human concerns—nothing special, but they were mine. Now, I didn't even know what any of this meant. Supposedly, I was still on Earth, but in some distant future city, and I had no idea how I got here or how to get back.

"By the way, have you eaten?" I tried to steer the conversation toward something mundane, hoping to give my scattered thoughts a break.

"Thank you for your concern, but I don't need to eat. Just as I created your meal, my body generates all the necessary substances for its proper functioning. That doesn't mean I don't occasionally enjoy something delicious, but I prefer indulging in fruit rather than heavy meals."

"That's terrible; you're missing out on so much in life. Sure, from my lazy perspective, preparing food is more of a chore, like brushing your teeth, but the act of eating is truly enjoyable."

"You know, from my perspective, you're the one missing out on so much," she said with a concerned smile. "Don't get me wrong, but to me, you're like a blind and deaf person trying to stumble through life."

"That hurt."

No one had ever described me as such a flawed being. Sure, I'd been called an idiot or worse many times, but we all hear that from time to time. Her opinion, however, was on a whole different level of humiliation. I realized she must have heard my thoughts; after all, she said she'd make her adjustments after breakfast. Her expression left no doubt—she knew exactly how I felt.

"I'm sorry. I didn't mean to hurt you. Here, everyone knows everything, and we naturally have a lot of distance from various matters. Sometimes it's hard to remember that you're different and, as a result, you have a naturally developed tolerance for everything around you. Maybe as an apology, I'll prepare a gift for you. I'm sure you'll like it."

A gift from someone with such advanced technology and abilities had to be something truly exceptional.

"Apology accepted," I said, excited about the surprise.

Maybe I could use this to get something more later. It was valuable information, but one look at Kaselin's face dispelled any hope. That wasn't going to work. I had to salvage this social misstep somehow.

"Unlike you, I know exactly where I'm from," I blurted out without thinking.

"I sincerely didn't mean to offend you. It's just a matter of perspective. You can't perceive energy, higher dimensions, spiritual beings, or even light beyond a very narrow spectrum, and you see space as something empty. I'm just trying to help you understand my perspective, and also the fact that we can't understand the differences between us and your origin. It's a huge mystery to us, and I'm not entirely convinced your theory is correct."

"Of course it's obvious—I'm from your distant past. Maybe your data is incomplete, which is why you can't determine when I'm from. And yes, this is Earth—your Earth, my Earth. And by the way, empty is empty; there's nothing in emptiness. Our physics has proven that long ago—case closed. Sure, you can put something in it, but on its own, it's empty."

I wanted to show her I was worth more than she thought. I was really hurt by what she had said.

"I experience space as almost a liquid energy that fills everything. A fluid that can be shaped—space itself is a form. You once had the concept of ether, but you assumed it was something purely physical, which was a mistake. There's no fluid or physical substance in a vacuum, yet it can be influenced, bent... If it were truly nothing, how could you shape it? How can nothing bend around a black hole's mass? How can nothing expand? Space is constantly expanding. Your scientists can observe quantum fluctuations, exotic particles from other densities that annihilate each other instantly because they're simply not meant to exist in such a low reality.

All of that is there—other dimensions, other densities— you just can't see it yet. Even from your theological perspective, you say God is everywhere. Do you really believe God is nothing? That something as powerful as God, being somewhere, wouldn't fill that space with its essence? Think about it—did a flat Earth become flat just because ancient people couldn't perceive it properly, or has it always been what it is, and humanity only discovered the truth over time?"

"I've already told you, I don't believe in God."

"Well, thank God that He still believes in you."

It all sounded like a fairy tale to me. Physicists had already proven that there is no ether, just a void. They had described and studied it—end of story.

"Until you can perceive a broader reality, you won't see the enormity that surrounds you."

"Maybe we should change the topic. This is like discussing grilling when you haven't even discovered fire yet. You said you know where you're from. Could you elaborate?"

"So, I'm from your distant past. It's the most logical option —a quick slice with Occam's razor and problem solved," I thought, proud of my wit and cleverness.

"We have a complete record from the moment this world was created by Lord Romasz and the Great Masters of Genetics. We know exactly what has happened since our inception. Our primary task is to care for His home and the Great Genetic Library of this galaxy, where every main genetic lineage is represented. We've never had the era you remember, and besides, you only have two helices in your DNA chain."

"Of course there are two—that's why it's called the double helix. How many do you think there should be? A hundred? This is basic knowledge, even kids in elementary school know that."

"Humans have 12 helices, which form more of a tube than a chain. This allows for encoding an enormous amount of information through more efficient packing and increased correlations in the genetic code.

Moreover, the shortening of telomeres at the ends of chromosomes during cell division by polymerase is such a fundamental flaw that no Master of Genetics would ever make such a mistake. Imagine how much this shortens your lifespan and your ability to accumulate experiences. It's unthinkable that something like that could have happened at all.

Your place of origin is a far greater mystery than just time travel from our distant past. A being like you has never existed, yet here you are."

I gave up—this was too much for me. I had no idea what she was talking about. Telomeres? Polymerase? I'm no chemist or biologist. I don't even know which branch of science to assign this to!

I needed to rest. Even though Kaselin was full of warmth and patience, it was all just too much. I had to calm down and gather my thoughts.

"I also have to go. There's a lot of work to be done. I'll leave you in peace, and I'll come by tomorrow to tell you what we've learned... If you need anything, just say it out loud, and the AI will assist you."

With that, she gave me a warm hug goodbye and left the house—or rather, the hallway, where the carport should have been. It turned out my apartment was created on a high floor of some enormous building.

As I said, it was all just too much. I needed to rest.

5 EVENING

I took a little nap. Thank God I didn't have any dreams. I slept deeply, although it was rather short—or at least it felt that way.

There was a book lying on the table. If this was the promised apology gift, I must admit I felt disappointed. There are so many wonders around me, technology bordering on magic, and she gave me a book? Just a plain book? Utter failure, in its purest form.

Without much enthusiasm, I picked it up and looked closer. There was nothing special about it—no advanced technology or hidden mechanisms. Just a plain book with an unappealing title: "The Most Powerful Affirmations Known to Humankind." Some kind of reality-bending nonsense straight from success coaches.

"I'm a winner!" I shouted sarcastically. But let's see what they're trying to sell us. Probably some nonsense that desperate people believe in to force themselves to do things they don't want to do, thinking it will guarantee happiness and fulfilment. Personally, I think if they stopped doing the things they learned in these success courses, they'd be much closer to this elusive happiness.

Desired results without effort—that's what everyone loves most.

A random page near the end—likely where the interesting parts are to hold the reader's attention. Let's see what we have here...

"I Am."

An infinite wisdom and love guide me in all things, along with the power of will and unceasing self-awareness.

I rejoice in my full power and full health, and within my body and mind, the law of harmony and light is at work.

Beauty, maturity, peace, understanding, and prosperity are forever mine.

My entire life is governed by principles of righteousness and Divine Order, as a result of which I fully develop all my abilities.

These truths are founded on the eternal laws of life, and so, wherever I go, I walk safely on the inspired path.

I know, feel, and believe that my beloved self manifests my conscious thinking faithfully to the smallest detail, and all that is in disharmony is immediately consumed in the eternal fire of forgiveness."

"I was right. Some psychological mumbo-jumbo, nothing of value. It's a real shame she didn't give me something genuinely useful in life, something that would help me move forward in this chaos and gain a better sense of understanding..."

It's pure audacity to say someone like me had no right to exist. Tell that to billions of people, if you're so smart. I lost interest in reading.

It was still daytime, and the AI turned out to be very helpful. It fulfilled every request I made. I've never eaten so much in my life, but since it was free, it would be a sin not to indulge.

I asked for the most expensive and exotic things I could think of, and I have to say, not everything deserved its reputation, but free is free.

I eventually ended up with a glass of fine whiskey on the sofa, feeling a bit tipsy, and absent-mindedly asked, "What do you guys watch on TV? I'm really curious what your news looks like."

"I can synthesize it into a television program."

"Whatever that means, show me what you've got," I said, and turned on the TV.

An enormous hall appeared on the screen, resembling some sort of parliamentary session or meeting, but with a huge number of members. The arrangement of the hall was also different. In the centre was a speaker and several figures, surrounded by a circle of people, one of whom would occasionally step forward, join the discussion, or announce something, and then return to their place. At the very centre was a man constantly present, wearing golden armour with purple accents. I could swear it was glowing with its own light. Actually, "armour" wasn't quite the right word—maybe more like a "suit," as it only covered his shoulders, torso, and knee-high boots. The rest of the outfit probably wasn't part of it. It was hard to tell from this distance. It looked grotesque but also pleasantly tickled my memories.

Dragon Ball—the essence of my childhood. Just behind the circle stood several warriors in similar covering, though not as radiant.

Around the entire central zone sat the main assembly, like at a soccer match. An uncountable crowd watched what was happening in the central part and smoothly emitted various colours, changing here and there but increasingly shifting toward one particular colour—the colour of one of the speakers.

The tall man in the armour was passionately talking about the need to raise the alert level and prepare for war. Some speakers urged for a show of force, while others felt that the current situation did not require further action. Few agreed to raise the banners and march to battle.

By the end, only the man and his interlocutor remained in the centre.

"The Dark Ones are raising their heads more and more and preparing for battle. There are fewer of them, but they are completely determined to strike," the tall man declared.

"We have a 10-to-1 advantage in the number of worlds. They don't pose as big of a threat as you claim," his interlocutor replied.

"Many of these worlds are completely pacifist. Not only will they be unable to join the war, but they will also need protection."

"For millions of years, the Dark Ones have been a threat, and for millions of years, the galaxy has lived in peace. We are a mixed galaxy, and we've always been proud of that."

"Now they are united under one banner and motivated to strike together. They've always feared confrontation, but united, they are more powerful than ever before. We've never faced such a large threat."

"Our standard fleets have always handled every threat, always neutralized local dangers. I see no reason why this time should be different..."

"This time it will be open war along the entire border—it won't be individual groups to be controlled. They will strike together, as one army..."

More and more of the crowd began to take on the colours of the man's opponent. Desperate, the man in the armour urged for action before it was too late—before the Dark Ones fully organized and used their power.

"You're a soldier, General, but subject to the decisions of this council, and as you can see, they have already decided. We will not start a war out of fear. We will not show weakness."

The vast majority of the assembly took on the colours of the General's opponent. The vote was over, the decision made...

The man bowed in resignation, and the entire circle returned the bow as he quickly and confidently walked away like a soldier. His entourage followed him in formation.

There was a certain dignity and strength in this. I could feel the power behind them—a power beyond my comprehension.

"Another drink, darling," I asked the AI, and as usual, it magically appeared on the table... Perfect...

I turned off the TV. Just regular politics. A lot of talking, and nothing changes anyway. Politicians talk, and yet it's always the same—or even worse. Some things, it seems, never change.

Kaselin was wrong. If you can't make yourself another drink, there's always AI to do it for you. Especially since the only thing I can make is in the bathroom, but let's not go there...

To pass the time, I asked the AI about the political debate, and to my surprise, it wasn't some local assembly but the Galactic Council. Interesting—humans had colonized the entire galaxy. So we are alone in the universe, or at least in our galaxy, but who are the Dark Ones? Some rebellious faction? Perhaps another race that inhabits our galaxy, though for obvious reasons, humanity dominates.

We are the best, I thought proudly. Never before had I felt such pride in our species. Honestly, it was probably the first time I ever felt proud of humanity—previously, I had no reason for it. The whole galaxy, or almost the whole galaxy, and who knows, maybe the entire universe? That's something to be proud of. Humans, rulers of the universe. It seemed obvious to me that we were so far into the future that it was no wonder they had no records from the very beginnings. 12-strand DNA—maybe it was some modification of the human genome at some stage of conquest?

They can learn so much from me about the origins of humanity. Maybe I'll even become someone important? Rich... I started to get sentimental, imagining my bright future. With each passing second, I became more important in my own eyes, more popular... Interviews, fame... The future looked so wonderful—alcohol certainly fuelled my imagination...

"Another one, darling."

I spent the rest of the day listening to music perfectly tuned to my intoxicated state, basking in the glow of this wonderful drink and the future that awaited me.

6 THE NEXT DAY

The next day, I woke up late, but considering the amount of alcohol I had consumed the previous night, I felt strangely refreshed and in a good mood. It's an amazing feeling to wake up without a hangover. I had never experienced anything like it. This alone made the day seem wonderful right from the start. But how long could I sit at home? This wasn't some kind of house arrest. I was surrounded by unimaginable wonders of this world, and all I had done was get drunk to the sound of music. I felt almost ashamed of wasting time that anyone I knew would probably give up their life for. Today, I would make much better use of my time. After all, I didn't know how long this adventure would last, and I had the feeling that a lifetime wouldn't be enough to see even a fraction of the wonders this incredible world had to offer.

With this noble resolution in mind, I began preparing breakfast. I was very hungry, and the quality of the food here seemed to score a 100 on a 10-point scale of taste. If this kept up, I would soon be the heaviest person on the planet. But somehow, that didn't bother me now. The food was worth its weight in gold.

"AI, when did humanity colonize this galaxy?"

"Humanity never colonized this galaxy. The primary task of humanity is to take care of Earth and the Great Galactic Genetic Library."

"What do you mean by taking care of the library?" "Earth was directly created by Lord Romasz and part of his siblings as their home in this galaxy. With the help of the Great Masters of Genetics, all major forms of life from our galaxy were gathered on its surface. And humans, as the caretakers of the planet, help others seeking knowledge in exploring the contents of the library."

"Got it. So, as the caretakers of God's house (only fools believe in him, but we can always use it), we have the most say and lead the galaxy, like ancient priests in Egypt led the common folk."

"There were only a few humans at the assembly, in your understanding of the term."

"But I saw it myself. There were hundreds of thousands of people at those galactic councils or whatever they're called."

"There were representatives of all the major races and members of the Galactic Council, the oldest races, who now primarily reside in the 5th density. For the sake of simplicity, they all appeared human to present a form understandable to you."

"Even AI thinks I'm an idiot. What a disaster. Oh, what a sight it would be to see everything as it truly is..."

I felt humiliated once again. The entire feeling of impending glory vanished in a split second...

It was insulting that even AI had reduced the message to a form it believed I could grasp. I hadn't even been given a chance to prove it wrong. I was capable of so much more, and there was no need to treat me like a child.

44

Knock, knock.

"May I come in?" I heard Kaselin's familiar voice.

"Sure, come on in," I said enthusiastically. I desperately needed a different conversational partner.

"I see you're enjoying some delicious treats. I'm glad your morning is going well. Honestly, if I were in your shoes, I'd be doing the same thing."

"Are you human?" I asked bluntly.

"Of course I am," she replied, surprised for the first time during our conversation.

"You're not lying? As far as I've learned here, you might not be, and I wouldn't even know it. So, are you human?"

"I am 100% human, flesh and blood."

"It's the first time I've seen you surprised—that's something new. Could it be that you're finally out of my head, or are you just pretending so I won't notice? That's the real question now."

"We have no need to lie. Besides, it's impossible when everyone around can see my thoughts. Even if I wanted to, others would immediately know. Such an act would be utterly pointless."

"But you don't communicate with thoughts like that little girl did."

"We agreed yesterday that I wouldn't do that, plus I've been speaking to you with words from the beginning so as not to increase the discomfort and stress you're already under. Your form of communication seemed the best way to help you."

"You often use the plural, but I'm only talking to you."

"A whole team is working on your case, and we're treating it as a priority. There are too many unknowns to ignore it."

"So, I'm here under special conditions?"

"It's our duty to help all beings here. Your case, however, is exceptional and incredibly difficult to resolve. Too many elements don't fit any known reality."

"That's true; it's hard to wrap my head around it all. This world is so vastly different from what I know, on so many levels. It's really hard for me to find my place here.

And I'm not just talking about the technological superiority, but the superiority in every imaginable way— and probably in ways I can't even comprehend."

"We understand that this is difficult for you. We can't grasp everything either. Our methods of analysing the situation have failed, which is why we've asked for help. When you're ready, a representative of an advanced race from the 5th density will come to see us."

It's a great honour to meet him. His civilization, billions of years ago, was responsible for seeding life in this galaxy and taking care of it in its early stages of development. He possesses far greater abilities than we do, and we believe that with his help, we'll be able to solve your case. We believe he will help us understand who you are and where you come from."

"But that's simple: I'm Johnny from Burton. No deeper understanding is required."

"From our perspective, the Earth you come from doesn't exist, nor has it ever existed. In any known reality, there is no such world as the one you remember. We can't comprehend it, which is why we've asked for help."

A civilization that is billions of years old? I couldn't even imagine such a span of time. So they were flying around the galaxy when there weren't even dinosaurs on Earth? What am I saying—maybe Earth itself didn't even exist?

Does that mean near-infinite development, or perhaps near-infinite stagnation? They seeded life in this galaxy, so does that mean there are older galaxies, and we're only in the early stages of development? How many such civilizations could there be?

Was it one of the first or one of many? Where are the others, and what was their task? And how many densities are there, anyway? It seemed that the universe was a far more fascinating place than I had ever imagined. My thoughts were interrupted by Kaselin.

"So, shall we invite him?"

"Fine, let him come," I replied resignedly. My musings hadn't led me to any meaningful conclusions. After all, what did we have to lose? "I just want to warn you that you're not accustomed to perceiving such beings. That's why he'll lower some of his energy so it can manifest in our third density, where you normally function."

"Do you mean the 3rd dimension? Are you saying he comes from another dimension?"

"Dimensions and densities are not the same thing. Even within the third density, there are many dimensions, but it's still the third density. He comes from a higher plane of existence, a very high one, which gives him far better insight into areas we don't have access to. One of those areas is the Akashic Records. Checking its records should greatly help in solving the mystery you present."

"The Akashic Records? That's new. Wouldn't it be easier to have the library and the records in the same place? Then you, too, could access it without asking others for help. Maybe it's worth considering?"

"The Records aren't a place you can just visit. I mean, you can visit them, but it's not that simple. It's more of a dimension, an area, a collection of vibrations—you can call it different things—existing beyond time and space, which is a record of all experiences of all beings, so your experiences will also be there."

"That must be an impressive place, but impossible to create. A record of EVERYTHING? That's simply impossible, no matter how advanced a civilization is."

"I wouldn't call it a place, but the ability to be there is indeed fascinating. But back to the topic—we're not sure how you'll perceive him. Part of you will sense his presence, and your brain will present him in a form most familiar to you. A bit like seeing familiar images when looking at clouds. That doesn't mean he will be that thing, but that you'll interpret him that way. Do you understand what I mean?"

"Of course I do."

I was tired of being treated like a halfwit, but honestly, I wasn't sure what she really meant. Does that mean I'll see a talking cloud? If I'm right, this might be quite an amusing experience.

"Remember, though, that he's here to help you. Whatever you see, he's your friend."

Was she trying to warn me about something terrifying? Images of the worst demons and monsters from various horror movies flashed through my mind. Almost immediately, I felt my heart race, and adrenaline flooded my veins. What if he himself is billions of years old? Anything that old must look awful. Maybe he would be horribly deformed or have some life-support apparatus around him? I braced myself for the worst.

I heard Kaselin in my thoughts inviting our guest, but what I saw knocked me off my feet. Even in 100 years, I wouldn't have imagined what I was about to see. Into the room walked a small green leprechaun in a funny tunic with a pot of gold on his back. I must admit, I didn't expect that, and I burst into hysterical laughter.

"Great Sir," I said with amusement in my voice. "Welcome to my humble abode."

All that was missing was for him to arrive via a rainbow and carry digging tools.

"Thank you kindly," replied the leprechaun. "I'm glad that out of all possibilities, you saw me in a form that improved your mood. I think for a first meeting, it went unexpectedly well."

"And how do you intend to conduct this examination? Will you be taking some samples? I've heard about alien abductions, and I'd be embarrassed to undergo some of those tests in front of Kaselin. But being examined by a leprechaun—that's another level of absurdity."

His thin, squeaky voice completed the absurdity of the whole situation. If I were to be examined by him, as tales of alien abductions suggest, I didn't think I was ready for something like that.

"Remember that it's only your way of perceiving, not the actual form of our esteemed guest. Please, let's maintain a bit of seriousness," said Kaselin with a clear expression of disapproval on her face.

For the first time, I saw Kaselin treating someone with a higher degree of respect. But then again, I'd never seen her in the company of anyone else, so I had no idea how she behaved around other people besides me. That made me wonder, and the amusement disappeared as quickly as it had appeared.

"No physical examination will be necessary, unless you very much prefer that form of testing," said the leprechaun with clear amusement. "All I need to do is read the frequency of your soul, and with that information, I'll search the Akashic Records."

"The frequency of my soul?" I asked with evident surprise. I didn't know that my soul had a frequency assigned to it.

"Every soul is a unique vibration of consciousness, unrepeatable and singular. Once you know these vibrations, you can always find such a soul and contact it, regardless of where it is manifesting at the moment. That's why someone with the appropriate abilities can find or contact a soul by having contact with something in which its vibration has imprinted. It can be an image, a memory, something created or written by that soul, a personal item.

By simply tuning into that vibration, you can contact the very consciousness that corresponds to it—that's all. In essence, it's very simple. Everyone has this ability to some extent. Often, we can have intuitions about someone because their vibration is somehow connected to us, and we can use it to make contact. Such an ability is possessed by almost all living creatures.

The combined vibrations of a given race form its chord, and all creatures together form a great orchestra of life. Each chord also has a common field of consciousness, being somewhat the resultant of individual sounds. Additionally, you can trace the path of a given soul by knowing its vibrations, and you can certainly check it in the Akashic Records since everything is recorded there. That's all the theory regarding my examination. I already know your vibration, and for now, that's enough for me."

The leprechaun bowed low. It seemed as if the heavy pot of gold didn't restrict his movements in any way. He turned on his heel and began to leave with a jaunty stride.

"I have everything I need. I'll immediately start the search," he said and exited.

"Now there's nothing left for us but to wait for what he finds. Maybe to pass the time, you'd like to visit Anatea? She asked about you and was very worried about your fate," Kaselin suggested.

"Ah... that strange girl who doesn't speak words." At the very thought of her, I felt uneasy again. The last time I was in her company, I experienced the worst panic attack of my life.

"She's just a child who cares about you and who perhaps saved your life by finding you. Besides, a little trip might be quite pleasant and take your mind off all those thoughts swirling in your head right now."

A trip sounded like something really promising. Even if its destination was that terrifying girl, what I would see along the way was mine to enjoy.

"Alright, after all, I have nothing better to do. Here, even the TV lies—sorry, adjusts information to my consciousness." That sounded smarter.

So basically nothing new; it's exactly like back home. Adjusting information to the recipient instead of just conveying the truth, and if the truth gets changed along the way, so much the worse for the truth.

"Okay, I'll pin a clasp to your clothes. I'll send you to her, and when you want to return, just press it, and it will instantly bring you back to your apartment."

"Wait a minute, you're talking about teleportation—you don't want to kill me, do you?" I got seriously scared!

"How would I kill you? I don't understand. I'll just transfer you to the place."

"I've read about this. It's murder. You'll kill me here and create some copy of me at the destination. Maybe the copy will be the perfect me, but I know full well that I won't be alive anymore. The fact that I won't see or remember that you're killing me doesn't mean you're not committing murder."

"I would never consciously harm you. It doesn't work that way, dear friend," she said with clear concern in her voice. "Let's say your body is a TV set, and your soul is the TV signal that permeates the entire universe.

Your soul tunes into your body during pregnancy, and from the moment of this tuning, it stays with it until the biological death of the organism. Moving the TV from place to place doesn't affect the TV signal in any way.

Even if you destroyed the TV in one place and recreated it in another, it wouldn't affect the TV signal, and it could still display freely on the TV. But don't worry; we won't be destroying anything—we'll just move you from one place to another. We have this technology really well developed."

"No, no, no, I'd rather not risk it. It would be better if I went to her by taxi. You have some form of taxi here, don't you?" I pondered this because it's not so obvious. Why would anyone need taxis if they can teleport in the blink of an eye?

"Alright then, I won't force you. I'll gladly arrange some transport so you can meet the heroine who saved your life."

"Yes, right, a heroine—a mere child."

"Maybe a mere child, but who knows—without that child, you might not be here now."

"Okay, you're right. I'd be happy to meet her and thank her for saving my life."

"Thank you, that's really kind of you. I'll arrange some transport shortly. Now, if you'll excuse me, I'll attend to my duties."

"Before you go, may I ask one question?"

"Sure, go ahead."

"It's hard to put into words, but is it really that bad?"

"Can you tell me more specifically what you mean? I respected your request to get out of your head, and now you need to express your thoughts a bit more precisely."

"I mean the Dark Ones and the fact that they pose a threat."

"Lord Romasz believes so, and he knows a lot."

"But since he's considered some kind of God, as you say, why don't others listen to him? Can't he just force them to obey instead of persuading them of his reasons?"

"What would free will be, if we were forced into something not of our own choice? He can persuade, but will certainly not force anything."

"But out of respect, shouldn't you listen to what he tells you?"

"I trust him implicitly, but perhaps the societies of this galaxy still have much to learn. It's not for me to judge. Maybe we're not as advanced as we think, and as a whole, we don't see certain obvious things? You know, we don't yet constitute such advanced civilizations as it might seem from your perspective, and probably we still have a long way of learning and experiences to gather. As I said, it's not for me to judge."

"You have much more humility than I thought."

"I've seen such wonders in my long life that despite theoretically understanding how they work, I'm still far from truly realizing what they really entail."

The sadness she left behind as she exited was almost physically palpable. Much more serious matters were happening than what I was being told. Does all this have something to do with me? I don't know, and I rather think not, but the heavy feeling remained in my heart. Who knows, maybe this trip will improve my mood.

No matter how advanced the universe is, there will always be someone who doesn't want to listen.

7 TAXI

It's been a few minutes since Kaselin left. I still can't shake off the feeling of deep sadness and worry she left behind, as if she knew something terrible was coming, and there was no way she could stop it.

Suddenly, the outer wall of my apartment turned into something liquid and transformed into a small bridge leading outside, straight to a small oval egg-shaped structure with an opening on the side of the bridge, inviting me in. I stood there dumbfounded for a moment, but with nothing else to do I headed toward the entrance. It was quite a challenge as we were hundreds of meters above the ground, but surprisingly, there wasn't the slightest wind that could threaten me in any way. It was as if I were in some invisible tunnel that perfectly shielded me from any atmospheric dangers expected at such a height.

I had no choice but to embark on my journey. Even though the vehicle outside seemed to be made from a single metal cast, inside all the walls were entirely transparent, with only one comfortable seat in the middle.

I almost had the impression that the chair was floating in the air, but I knew it was attached to the base of this strange egg-shaped vehicle, which in some ways seemed eerily familiar.

No window could provide a view like this. I could look in any direction without any limitations. I felt almost as if I were sitting in a magical chair, floating in the air. I felt like a small child, excited about the upcoming journey. I was sure I would witness wonders that even the greatest philosophers hadn't dreamed of.

The vehicle suddenly moved at great speed, rising above the city. I didn't feel any acceleration, no discomfort, not even my ears popped from the rapid gain in altitude. It felt as if I was sitting in the chair with the rapidly changing scenery projected around me. No G-forces—it was incredible. But that was nothing compared to the view unfolding before me.

The city was enormous, absolutely massive. London, by comparison would be a small settlement. Beautiful towering buildings rose above the city, and between them various smaller and larger objects zipped around with unknown purposes. I didn't see any streets, and the whole area between the buildings was filled with gardens and parks. Walking through them were such diverse creatures that even if you gathered all the imagination of humanity, we couldn't come up with such a vast array of species and forms that I could now admire from within my taxi.

Although we were flying at a relatively low altitude, I didn't notice any markings or traffic organization. It was as if some invisible force was controlling the entire chaos, allowing everyone to move without any hindrance.

We began to ascend higher and higher at incredible speed. We had to be very high, really high, as it felt like we were leaving the atmosphere. Above us, in space, thousands of ships of various shapes and sizes floated.

From small units to gigantic ones that could serve as large cities on their own. All the shipyards of the world wouldn't be able to build even one of them, yet there were many of these massive colossi here. The power of Earth seemed limitless. I had never seen anything so monumental and yet so beautiful at the same time.

"This is incredible, what the human race has achieved," I said to myself out loud.

"Most of the ships around us don't belong to Earth's fleet but to races that want to benefit from the great library. They send their larger or smaller expeditions to conduct their necessary research. It's also an excellent place for exchanging experiences and establishing contacts with other races. After all, we are the true jewel of this galaxy."

I was speechless—there were so many ships gathered in various orbits, providing enough space for everyone. Layer upon layer, so diverse in both size and form. The space around the planet was teeming with different ships, a stark contrast to the typical void of space. It all looked like something out of a movie. This phenomenon didn't appear to be localized—everywhere, there was the same activity, the presence of various races eager to visit this place.

"There must be far more people here than on the planet's surface."

"Not necessarily humans, as other species make up the vast majority, but you're right. There are many more beings in orbit than on the planet's surface. Earth couldn't fulfill its role if everyone were allowed to visit the surface. They would ruin the entire genetic wealth, which is the true treasure of this planet. Only research groups and representatives of the visiting races can go to the surface. Everyone else must stay in orbit to respect their hosts. But don't worry—they're quite comfortable up there, and we provide them with everything they need."

"Earth must be an incredibly rich world if so many civilizations are using its services."

"We are home to Lord Romasz. We can create everything we need and what our guests require, and many civilizations gladly support us technologically or otherwise in gratitude or respect. However, we provide all resources and the content of the library for free. It's a great honour to share this knowledge, and it would be dishonourable to demand anything in return."

"This Romasz—is he the god you worship?"

"He is the builder of this planet and the father of its soul. He is one of the seven chosen to oversee this universe. They are the ones who manifest the will of the God Creator. They ensure that His will is smoothly implemented in the lower worlds. They also watch over everything and care for all creation within their responsibilities."

"You know, I don't really believe in God. Especially not one with children—who would He have them with? That part really amuses me. If He's the Father of His children, then logically, there must have been a mother."

"He didn't sire them. You're reducing to your level a power you don't understand. He simply brought the entire seven into existence by an act of His will to fulfill the tasks assigned to them."

"Or everything happened by chance, which is far more likely than some God who created everything. Where did He come from? The theory of chance is much more probable."

"That would have to be an incredibly lucky chance for everything to align in such minute detail. All aspects aligned so perfectly that even the smallest change would cause everything to fall apart.

Take, for example, your eye. Even minor changes in the eyeball, and you wouldn't see as well. Slightly larger changes, and you wouldn't see at all, yet it would still resemble an eyeball."

"It's just evolution, nothing more. First, individual cells mutated, failed attempts died off, and in the end, fully formed eyes emerged."

"Evolution is a clever name for a process whose genius you don't really understand. Are you aware that the brain has to analyse, create the appropriate areas, learn to operate them, and establish connections with the eyes? The eyes themselves must be formed almost perfectly to function. The pupil, rods, everything must be in perfect harmony.

Many species don't evolve for hundreds of millions of years, only to evolve into a new species within a few."

"For you, it's evolution; for me, it's planned genetic action."

"It happens because environmental conditions change. It's proven that it occurs based on a natural process. The stronger, more adapted individuals pass on their traits, and everything changes."

"And that's why all species develop so consistently, because chance rules, and it's not directed by some higher intelligence? And maybe you'll also tell me that instinct is not a manifestation of consciousness but mechanical reacting? How can ants accidentally learn to cooperate so well without a shared field of consciousness that knows how to manage them all so that something coherent emerges?"

"Because that's how instinct and evolution work. It just works because it developed that way, and it doesn't need to be guided by some higher intelligence."

"I think we won't reach an agreement on this issue. I believe there are no coincidences, and you think everything is a coincidence. I guess we'll have to agree to disagree."

"Okay, changing the subject. If God is the god that religion says He is, omnipresent, why would He need a home? Maybe it's just manipulation for the masses, something that can be used for personal gain. In the past, many religions exploited the naivety of the faithful for power, wealth, influence, or just the pleasure of being an elite among the little people."

"I don't know if He or any of His siblings need a home, but living beings need a tangible place for His presence. And earth is that place. It is the jewel of this galaxy, sharing its knowledge with all."

"Even with the Dark Ones?"

"They're not looking for the kind of knowledge we have to offer."

"So who exactly are they?"

"They are civilizations mired in darkness, cruelty, and the desire for as much power as possible. They don't recognize the law of unity but the law of strength and conquest."

"So, just regular barbarians. They must be so backward that they don't pose a threat to such a power."

"Their technologies are very advanced, but they are focused on gaining military superiority. That's their main and primary goal—to dominate everyone else."

"Then why not just exterminate them? We could wipe them out and have peace. We have the numerical advantage, after all."

"They are also fragments of God's consciousness, but they elevate their own divinity above the divinity of others.

They are entirely focused on themselves. We serve the fragments of God around us, and by doing so, we grow ourselves, helping each other. They elevate their fragment often by demeaning everyone else around them. Our domain is love and understanding; theirs is cruelty and domination, but we are all created by God and have the right to live."

"Why help the particles of God, if they are divine?"

"You are one yourself. Consciousness is God. Your consciousness, your soul, is a tiny fragment of His essence. Like drops of water in the ocean. Each drop contains everything the ocean holds."

"I'm God? That's new. If I'm so powerful, then why can't I do everything?"

"Your consciousness is of divine origin. You have all of His attributes within you, but you don't remember. In your essence, you yourself have the potential to create universes."

"I can already imagine it. Humanity creating universes. I can see how that would end."

"Fortunately, before you develop such abilities, much time will pass during which you will gain wisdom and experience. However, you do have this potential, that is certain, everyone does, but you simply don't remember. And because everyone around you also comes from the same source, from a certain perspective, they are us, on a different path of experience. By helping them, we help ourselves, and we also grow. This is the law of unity. The law of selfless love."

"It doesn't make sense to me. Why forget everything if you already knew it all? That doesn't add up. It's like being at the finish line right at the start. So why take the whole journey? It would be better not to move at all and have everything already.

Dream job, best results without doing anything. It doesn't fit together at all. Just another fairy tale for the masses to keep them under control."

"I'm afraid we need to end our conversation, we're approaching the landing. The destination is near those buildings."

Once again, I missed so much, focusing on this unproductive conversation instead of admiring everything we passed along the way. I concentrated too much on trying to prove my companion wrong, and after all, it's just the AI of this taxi. Who would care about convincing a mere computer program? I wasted precious time again.

The whole trip must not have taken that long, but here the sun was already setting. We had to cross several time zones in less than half an hour. It's incredible how quickly we travelled.

8 THE PICTURE

The ship gently landed on a clearing near some building. I thanked the AI for the ride and headed toward Anatea, who was painting something on a canvas and seemed unaware of our arrival. The area looked mostly like meadows, with a few larger clusters of trees here and there. It reminded me a lot of my country, except instead of meadows, there were fields of crops everywhere. I walked slowly toward the girl, who greeted me cheerfully without turning around, still completely absorbed in her painting.

"I was worried about you," she said without speaking. "You looked terrified and lost consciousness. Fortunately, grandma and grandpa were nearby, and we managed to call for help quickly. Are you feeling better now?"

"Grandma and grandpa? Where are your parents?"

"Mum's a biologist and takes care of the local species, making sure they don't lack anything, and Dad serves on an escort ship belonging to Lord Romasz's personal guard. It's a great honour to serve in it," she said with undisguised pride.

"Aren't your parents supposed to be with you, raising you, and taking care of you when you need them? Isn't that the parents' duty?"

"My parents are always with me when I need them, and we often play together, but they also have important work to do and spend a lot of time on it. My grandparents are always nearby, and as Mum says, they have much more wisdom and patience, so it's natural they take care of me more often. My grandparents are really great and know so much. All my friends have great grandparents who play with them. Was it different for you?"

"Usually, parents take care of the children; after all, they're their children."

"Didn't your parents have important work to do?"

"No, they worked a lot."

"Then how could they be with you if they were working a lot?"

"I was often home alone; that's just how it was."

"That's strange. If you lived with your grandparents, you would never have had to be alone. It's so sad that they weren't with you."

"But parents are the closest family, they're the most important."

"Grandparents are family too, and it gives parents time to do adult things. Grandparents have already done their work and can now just play. They have lots of time to play and are so wise. They know everything and have time to explain it all. I love them very much, just like I love Mum and Dad. It's great that we're all one family."

I didn't want to continue down this line of thought. Raising children by an older, more patient, less busy generation with much more experience made a lot of sense, but it clashed with my idea of responsibility for children. Even if there wasn't enough time to do adult things and take care of the children, causing them to miss out on what they truly needed, I couldn't fully agree. I wasn't even going to mention single mothers, who, though they supposedly had more time, still saw their family circle reduced. Grandparents were, in many ways, better suited as caregivers and it strengthened family bonds, but it clashed so much with my own understanding of parental responsibility that I couldn't accept it. I quickly changed the subject.

"What are you painting?"

"It's the universe," she replied proudly. "Grandma loves it when I paint. She always likes it and proudly shows my work to all her friends. Grandpa often teaches me cool tricks on how to make things look nice. He recently told me that when I paint trees, I should place the branches in the order of 1, 1, 2, 3, 5, 8, and 13 branches, and then it will look just right. He's so wise."

"And what's the difference in how many branches a tree has? A tree is a tree."

"But the tree knows how many branches it should have, and I should know too if I want to paint it properly. When I paint people, they have two hands, not seven, because that would look strange. It's the same with trees. I don't want to paint strange trees, I want them to be nice."

"So, if you want to paint the universe as it really is, it should have an elliptical structure, with clusters of galaxies and empty regions placed on it."

I wanted to be seen as a very wise adult too, and this advice was excellent. Even a little child would appreciate it.

"It's a map of the universe of living species. Mum showed me a simulation like this, and I tried to remember it well. It was very colourful and really, really beautiful. I think it's roughly right... I think..."

"But it looks like a colourful blot where the colours flow smoothly into each other. What does this have to do with the universe?"

"It's obvious. Similar species live close to each other. It's a great gift from a loving God to help us make friends easily. Similar ones live close, and the different ones live far away, which makes it easier to play together. Everybody knows that."

"Then what are the Dark Ones doing here? Shouldn't they be similar?"

"But they are similar, they just think differently. But they also have two hands and two legs. In our entire galaxy, almost everyone has two hands and two legs because God is good."

"They're a threat, and that means they should be isolated or destroyed. Showing mercy will only cause problems."

"How can you say such horrible things? They are also us, they're family, they just remember very little and have distanced themselves from who they are. They're lost, and we need to help them. Hug them, invite them to play, and maybe over time, they'll see that it's better to be kind than to be scary."

"I think we have to be tough."

"Maybe you're lost too, like the Dark Ones. I can hug you, because this way, everyone would be afraid of each other. Have you never had a friend who was mean to you at first, but later turned out to be your best friend?"

"That's different."

"Why?"

"Because not every adult can be your friend."

"Maybe so, I don't understand everything yet, but I know that there's a piece of God in everyone, even in the Dark Ones. They're not that different from us, they just don't understand."

"I see that your grandparents live in a very picturesque place. There's probably not much to do here."

"Oh no, there's plenty to do. All of humanity takes care of the great library, and I help with it as best I can," she replied proudly. "It's our great task for the good of the entire Galaxy." Her eyes shone with a strange light as I heard her words in my head.

"Don't you have to go to school? You're probably old enough to be learning important things with other children."

"Every day, I spend a few hours with a teacher who develops my hidden talents," she said proudly. "He says that one day I'll be a great artist because what I create has a soul, that I open people's hearts to their inner spark, and that it helps them find it more easily," she replied with great joy. "I've always felt that helping others is my destiny."

"And what about subjects you don't like?"

"I only learn them as much as necessary. Focusing on unnecessary things kills joy, our innate uniqueness. That's what my teacher says. I would probably die if I had to study more than necessary of that dreadful maths. I don't think I like it, but it's okay, there's not much of it. Unlike my friend, he almost only has mathematics. I really feel sorry for him, but he says he likes it. He's a bit strange sometimes, but I like him a lot. I think everyone is unique, even if they like maths and physics, and together we know everything. I can make beautiful drawings, our house would be very empty without them.

No one wants to live in a sad house, so I draw for everyone; it's a very important job," I again felt immense pride radiating from the girl.

"When you have to pay bills, there's not always time for beautiful things."

"What are bills?"

"You have to work to get what you need."

"Can't you just create it?"

"I can't," I admitted with genuine sadness in my voice.

"That must be a sad life, doing things you don't like."

"That's life. We don't always do what we want."

"That's a shame because if you did something you liked, you'd probably be really good at it. Maybe you just haven't found it yet and just need to look a little?"

I didn't want to admit to her that, in fact, I had never really looked for it. That my life had somehow just happened. It just turned out that way and stayed that way. Doing what you like seemed childish to me, doing what you don't like is a sign of adulthood. But this little girl didn't understand that yet, she was just a child.

"Maybe I'm just a child, but I know that if a flute pretends to be a violin, it'll make a lousy orchestra. That's what Grandpa always says, and he knows everything."

I had forgotten that everyone here could read minds. It's a frightening world where we have no privacy. Even a little girl hears more than the eavesdropping done by big corporations, supposedly for our good, to tailor advertisements for us. As if there weren't much better reasons to eavesdrop—supposedly for our own good, they spy on us. Funny how, when they can profit from us, our well-being takes a back seat.

"But if you don't know what to choose in life, how do you know if you're heading in the right direction if you don't know where to go?"

"Every direction is good if it lets you live well. The most important thing is to earn money without overworking yourself."

"But that's a terrible waste of life. It's like going to school and attending the wrong classes. How can you not know what you want to learn?"

"You learn everything."

"If I had to learn mathematics instead of drawing, I would be very sad, and I'd be terrible at maths because I brought with me talents for drawing. If I didn't know that I wanted to learn to share joy through my drawings, I'd be very tired and sad."

"So you knew what you wanted to do before you were born?"

"Of course, it's the only way I could bring the talents to learn what my spark wanted to learn. There has to be a plan, otherwise life would be very hard."

I was about to say something, but I heard someone calling. Or rather, thoughts intruding into my mind that could be called a call.

"Anatea, come home quickly, it's time to say goodbye to Dad."

"I have to go. I still want to show Dad my newest drawing before he goes on an important mission. I'm sure he'll like it," she said, quickly gathering her things and heading towards the house.

"Take care, John, I hope we meet again." She waved and ran to the house.

Sweet girl, but she still has a lot to learn about life. I couldn't believe I had been so afraid of her. She's just a girl who has a long way to go before becoming an adult. Things don't always turn out the way you want, that's life.

I wonder what this important mission is. They probably say that every time to make goodbyes easier. Parents often lie to their children for their own good.

I decided to take a walk around the area. Everything looked so normal, nothing suggested that I was so far in the future. Except for the fact that, wherever I looked, I could see a road with cars or some human activity, but here, apart from a few buildings, there was no unnatural activity.

I walked for a long time, enchanted by the beauty of the nature around me, wondering what my life would have been like if I had followed my passions instead of just mechanically performing my duties. It's not my fault that my life turned out this way; it just is what it is. There's nothing I can do about it. But had I ever even tried? Bills, loans—in the adult world, there's no time for childish things.

Suddenly, from a distance, I saw a glowing object quickly approaching me. It was my taxi. I didn't know it glowed while flying. It was probably a kind of signal, like on aeroplane.

It stopped silently a few meters away, and the familiar doors, or rather an opening in the egg, appeared, inviting me inside to sit in the familiar seat.

"Hurry, my friend, we have to go back. We don't have much time. We need to report to the capital as soon as possible."

I didn't understand the rush. If my presence there was so important, why did they let me go on a trip? It didn't make much sense, but the nervousness in the voice definitely urged haste. No one here got nervous.

The ship silently sped off at an incredible speed, much faster than when we travelled to the destination. I could literally see the stars moving along the sky in the opposite direction of our flight. How fast were we going for the stars to move along the sky like that? I had no idea what the answer could be.

"Do you know what's going on? Why the sudden hurry?"

"I have no idea; they didn't have time to explain, but I know that time matters."

"How can AI have no idea? Can't you check some database or send a query to some central system?"

"I'm Kaselin's assistant; why did you think I was AI?"

"There's no one here but me. How can you be a person and not part of the ship?"

"You mean to say you can't see me? I thought all humans could see higher densities."

"Apparently, I'm the only one who doesn't see as much as others."

"Sorry, I didn't know. If I had known, I would've lowered my vibration to a level visible to you."

"I've had enough of leprechauns with gold for one day."

– Leprechaun? Never mind. We'll be arriving shortly.

In the distance, the glowing lights of a massive city began to appear. The vehicle drastically slowed down, as the stars stopped shifting across the sky, but our speed was still far beyond the sound barrier. The city loomed ahead, growing rapidly.

It was unbelievable that we managed to avoid colliding with anything on the way—likely thanks to a pre-planned flight path designed by someone else. In any case, we quickly arrived at my residence, coming to a stop without any noticeable deceleration. The piloting skill bordered on magic, but I had no time to dwell on it. Inside, Kaselin was already waiting for me, accompanied by a peculiar-looking dwarf.

"The Lord Romasz himself will meet with you," Kaselin said with excitement in her voice. "You'll head straight to his flagship for the meeting."

"Did you discover something interesting about me?"

"Of course. The Akashic Chronicle never fails. That's why it's so important for you to meet him while there's still time."

"Time for what? I thought gods could do anything, so time shouldn't be an issue for them."

"There's no time for a long explanation. Lord Romasz is waiting. My assistant will take you to him, and we'll talk once you return."

With a wave of her hand, she gestured toward my taxi, her expression making it clear that there was no room for refusal.

Almost mechanically, I boarded the taxi. I didn't understand the gravity of the situation, but I knew that whatever was happening now was crucial. If their so-called god wanted to meet me, maybe I was more important than I realized.

9 LORD ROMASZ

This time, my taxi shot straight up into the sky. Within seconds, we reached orbit and began passing a massive fleet of visitors to Earth before heading directly into space, supposedly to Lord Romasz's flagship. In the next few seconds, Earth practically disappeared from sight. We sped up even more. The Sun shrank to the size of a distant star in the night sky. Even if we had reached the speed of light, it couldn't have happened so quickly. I had heard of Warp drives, which warp space to seemingly exceed the speed of light, but I doubted that such a small object could warp space. As humanity, we know so much, yet I couldn't grasp the principles behind the workings of a simple taxi.

"No one's ever called me a taxi driver," I heard a familiar voice in my mind.

"Sorry, I didn't mean to offend you."

"It's fine. It's actually kind of funny. As an assistant, I do everything that the great ones don't have time for, so I can also play the role of a taxi driver."

"But how is it possible that I don't feel any G-forces, even though we're going so fast?"

"Gravity, like any other force in the universe, can be controlled with the right technology. You can isolate its effects or generate your own as needed. It's not as hard as it seems once you understand what it's about.

The same applies to space or time, and right now, we're only talking about three-dimensional reality."

"I see," I replied, though in truth, I understood very little of what he had said.

"As you move up through dimensions or densities, more general laws come into play. The speed of light is a specific rule of this three-dimensional reality, within generally accepted interdimensional laws. As you probably guess, specific rules also take a more general form, like the laws of physics."

This explanation didn't really clarify anything. I still didn't know if they bypassed the speed of light through multi-dimensionality, if the taxi warped space to make us seem faster, or if they used something entirely unknown to me. But it didn't matter. I didn't ask for further explanations, as I likely wouldn't understand them anyway. I regretted not having studied astronomy more closely. Maybe then I'd know if we were still in the solar system or far beyond it. But one thing was certain: I was farther from Earth than any human of my time. Too bad no one would record this somewhere. It would be great to go down in history, to be someone famous, perhaps even have schools teach about me or have a building named after me. It would be nice to be remembered and recognized by the masses.

It seemed we were approaching our destination, as I could almost physically feel the excitement of my driver, pilot, astronaut, assistant... whatever I should call him. If he had been a simple AI, things would be a lot simpler.

Ahead of us loomed a massive ship, more resembling a work of art than a warship. In fact, I had no idea what starship flagships looked like—I had never seen one before. I couldn't estimate its size, as I had no point of reference to compare it with. But the large combat ships appearing out of nowhere looked like small fishing boats next to an aircraft carrier in comparison to this giant. The power and majesty of this vessel were unimaginable.

"You can tell right away that Arcturians were involved in designing this marvel," said the assistant. "They design everything like it's a work of art. Even if you have no taste at all, you instinctively feel that every detail has deeper meaning."

"Arcturians?" I asked, clueless.

"You're joking, right? They're one of the most powerful and ancient races in the universe. How could you not have heard of them?" the assistant replied, clearly surprised. "Everyone knows them. Everyone in the entire universe knows who they are. Theoretically, there might be places where they haven't been heard of, but in practice, I've never come across such a place... Actually, that would explain why you don't know. We don't know about each other. But that doesn't make sense, everyone knows them. This doesn't make sense. There must be an explanation. Where did you say you were from?"

"I was born on Earth."

"No, that doesn't make sense."

It was obvious that the idea that someone might not know about the Arcturians was beyond my companion's capacity for reasoning. He was stuck in his thoughts, presenting counterarguments to his own theories. Working with him every day probably involved some interesting challenges.

"Never mind, we've received permission to dock on board. We're approaching for landing."

"You're going to crash us!!!" I shouted in total panic. "Get a grip! You're flying straight into the side of the ship!"

Suddenly, we passed through the solid metal wall as if it wasn't there.

"An illusion? A hologram? A cloaking device to hide the hangar entrance?" I muttered, dazed, unable to believe we were still alive.

"A simple phase shift of our, as you call it, taxi allows us to bypass atomic interaction. After all, it's mostly empty space, and you can easily pass through it. Phase shifting objects is a handy technology. Creating entry gates would weaken the outer structure. This way is much easier. Didn't you know that either? So, where are you really from?"

"I already told you, from Earth. You know I'm telling the truth."

"I don't get it, but it explains why I'm the one driving," he concluded sadly.

"I really know how you feel. I've been feeling that way constantly lately," I tried to console him, but it seemed my words only made things worse.

I wasn't sure if our taxi had been phase-shifted or if the ship itself had been, but I knew I almost had a heart attack, a stroke, or who knows what else, watching us fly straight into that wall of strange metal. What mattered was that we were inside, safe and sound, and that's all that counted. Slowly, I started to calm down.

After stepping onto a huge platform, I didn't even have time to look around. Suddenly I was transported before a large, ornately decorated door, inscribed with unknown symbols.

The door stood in a long corridor, whose far end wasn't visible. Two guards in the familiar glowing armour stood before it. One of them easily opened the massive door and announced my arrival to the people inside. To my great relief, there were no dwarves. The enormous hall I entered was shrouded in semi-darkness, and the walls were covered with three-dimensional plastic images that I couldn't comprehend. A group of about a dozen people in glowing covering stood in the middle of the room, gazing at an image in its centre. Among them, I recognized the man who had tried to warn everyone at the meeting the day before about the impending threat from the dark ones. The intense concentration was evident on everyone's faces. Whatever they were discussing, it had to be something exceptionally difficult, as the heavy atmosphere was palpable. The seriousness of the situation was overwhelming. I stood there, as if hypnotized, waiting for someone to notice me.

"That's all, gentlemen. Go to your divisions and relay the orders. Precision and surprise are our main weapons in this battle."

"Yes, General," the others replied, and vanished, as if they had never been there.

"Come closer, please. We have a moment to talk."

"So, you're the one they consider a God. To me, you look like an ordinary human, not an all-powerful being."

"Everything is a matter of perspective and the level from which you view it. To you, I'm human, but probably to everyone, I'm something slightly different."

"Come closer, please. We have a moment to talk."

"So, you're the one they call God. To me, you look like an ordinary person, not an all-powerful being."

"Everything depends on perspective and the level from which you view it. To you, I am a human, but probably to everyone, I am something slightly different."

"Everyone believes what they want to believe."

"That's true, regardless of what that truth objectively is."

"So, are you God or not?"

"Imagine the sun, from which light originates. Its rays travel through space to reach the Earth and eventually fall on a glass of water. The purer the water in the glass, the more the original light shines through. I am the sun, which, in its frequency, fills the entire universe and all densities.

I am the rays of that sun, which permeate the other frequencies of existence across the entire spectrum of their being. I am also the light that pierces through the glass, my physical, local emanation of my essence. So, am I just an ordinary glass? Or the rays travelling through space? Or the sun itself shining in that glass? In a sense, I am all three of these aspects. What you see depends on your personal perspective, on the observer. Each answer is equally valid and will be your truth. So, you must answer for yourself whether I am God or human."

I didn't know what to say. I hadn't expected the conversation to take this turn at all.

"And what is your task?"

"I am the force that gently pushes all the sparks of the Creator God toward discovering their own divinity. I am the inspiration and motivation to walk toward oneself. I penetrate all densities and understand that everyone is important in the Great Plan of the Creator. I am also the Shield and the Sword, ensuring balance in the universe and that everyone has the right to develop according to their path."

"So, what is this path ultimately about?"

"On one hand, it's about raising your own consciousness, because by doing so, the water in your glass is purified, and you increasingly express who you truly are."

"But since we are this light from the start, why do we forget everything? Life would make much more sense if we were already a purified vessel. Life seems pointless when we could just as well remember everything from the beginning."

"It doesn't work quite like that. In the first universes, the first creations of the first generation of Creator Gods, the incarnated beings had full awareness of who they were (parts of God and simultaneously Gods), and they had no motivation to act. It didn't matter what happened to them or if they survived at all. They didn't develop in the way we understand development, because they were already at the end of the developmental process. This didn't create wisdom; it didn't lead to a deeper understanding of themselves. It created long-lasting, boring stagnation, where nothing developed because there was no reason for it... That's why the Great Forgetting was introduced."

"It's one thing to have the wisdom of all the cookbooks, and another to savour a delicious meal. It's one thing to have all the knowledge about cars, and another to enjoy driving on an empty highway. Omniscience and wisdom are attributed to all children of God, but it's experience that gives them their depth and value. To be truly amazed by something, you cannot remember everything, because then that depth would become very shallow."

I didn't know what to say. Deep down, I felt he was right, but I also felt as though I had been stripped of my entire heritage without my consent. Life is truly unfair.

"Life itself wasn't designed to be fair. How could you learn the power of forgiveness if no one ever wronged you? But nothing happens without your knowledge and consent, you just don't remember it.

Each life is designed to give you what you need, but unfortunately, not what John needs, but what your spark needs—to experience, to learn, and to grow. How could you deeply marvel at something or be truly surprised if you knew what would happen? How could you experience deep, wise love if you didn't place that experience in the context of its various shades and opposites? Your destiny is to grow and discover your true origin. To discover who you truly are."

"Yes, I've heard that somewhere before, supposedly we are all Gods, but I don't see how that's possible."

"Imagine a tiny segment on an infinite line. No matter how small that segment is, you can divide it into an infinite number of further segments, and those, in turn, into more infinities. At the core of your being, you are truly an individualized infinity surrounded by infinity. You have all the attributes of your Creator, and one day you will learn to express them."

I didn't know where this conversation was headed, what its purpose was, but another question that had been bothering me for a while was on my lips, and this was a great opportunity to voice it.

"It's obvious that I come from some distant past, technology wasn't as advanced yet, so doesn't my presence here affect the timeline? In movies, such things always end badly."

"The nature of time is actually multi-layered, or rather multi-dimensional. Let's say we compare it to a computer game you like to play.

Being at the level of the game character, you can embody it and experience planned adventures, even creating paradoxes, being in apparent danger, but from the higher level of the player, time remains consistent, and there are no paradoxes.

The character in the game, even if it goes back in time and kills its own grandfather, from the player's perspective, it's still a continuation of the game, time still flows linearly, and there is no paradox. You can play the game in different ways, restart it, go back in time, make all sorts of changes. The grandfather paradox is a paradox of time from the level of the game, but from the player's level, it's still a consistent timeline, and that's just the beginning of the adventure. Time is a multi-dimensional matrix, and its true depth is hard to explain."

"In practice, everything is happening now, yet simultaneously everything is happening sequentially. The fact that you're here doesn't disrupt anything. The fact that you're here is important."

"But how are we supposed to ascend, to purify our glass, bottle, or jug, however you want to call it—how are we supposed to play this game if no one explains anything to us?"

"You are never truly alone. I and others watch over you. Deep down in your heart, you feel what is right. Deep down, you know what should be done. You don't always make the best choices, but that's what this great adventure is all about. That's what learning is about. You are gently encouraged in the right direction, but it's up to you to choose it.

Abandoning any part of God would be like abandoning Him, you are never alone on your path, and the entire universe will come to your aid if only you ask. God is love, and He will NEVER stop loving you."

"That sounds really good, but in practice, it's just a nice theory that doesn't really help. I've called out so many times and never received an answer."

"You've always received an answer, we've always been with you, but you haven't always been able to see it."

"So, in practice, it doesn't help at all. What's the difference if there's no help or if I can't see it? I still feel alone. There are so many religions, so many viewpoints as there are people on the planet. Why aren't there universal rules for everyone to follow simply?"

"And where would free will be in that? Experimentation? If everything were predetermined, this entire experience would lose its meaning."

"Nonsense, all religions say that if I make the wrong choice, God will send me to hell. Where's free will if, by making the wrong choice, I'm punished so severely?"

"God loves you. It doesn't matter whether you make good or bad choices, He will still love you. Your choices affect the purity of your glass, but even in the darkest sludge, your light will still be there, and God will never stop loving it. How can the purest love and wisdom reject a small child for wanting to learn, for stepping beyond its limits, and bravely taking its first steps? Courage is not the absence of fear and perfect action. Courage is acting despite doubt and mistakes. They might be painful, but one day you will learn to run, and then it won't matter. What will matter is that, in the end, you succeeded. Who you truly are is always safe. No matter how terrifying the game may be, the player is always safe. You will never lose your heritage, your origin. You cannot lose what you've always had, even if you temporarily forget it."

"And how does karma fit into all of this? It's going to haunt me for a very long time. I'm not proud of everything I've done in my life. If God doesn't punish me, karma surely will."

"Imagine that karma is a kind of inertia from your experiences that pushes you with its momentum in a certain direction, like a pendulum that swings in all directions.

Let's say, for example, it represents financial matters. In the first scenario, you are full of altruism and give away everything you have (the pendulum swings to one extreme), but you die in poverty."

"In the next approach (the momentum of the pendulum swings to the opposite extreme), and now richer in experience, you don't share anything, and you die wealthy but lonely. Over time, you will learn the wisdom of sharing, and your pendulum will no longer push you in either direction. It will calm down somewhere in the middle. You will find the golden path of balance, and that lesson will be complete. The force of karma, the force of the pendulum, will no longer affect you in that aspect because it will no longer be necessary. And so, as you journey through various lessons, you go through the great labyrinth called life."

"The great labyrinth?"

"The great labyrinth of your self-perceptions. Your ideas of who you are replace the truth about you, but you are unaware of it. You are God, with the power to create anything you desire, anything you deeply believe in. Even if it involves difficult experiences. The spark of God that you are is, through forgetfulness, trapped in its own perception of itself. Your spark has its individuality, vibration, uniqueness, but instead of expressing it, you believe in your own vision of yourself, rather than in who you truly are. You call it ego, I call it the dream of the dreamer, the fluid in the glass that ultimately colours the eminence of your spark's light. The ego defends itself from the truth of who it really is because discovering the truth means transformation, awakening. Although the fluid in the glass colours the light, ultimately, the light always prevails and expresses itself fully. Even though the dream doesn't truly exist, from a certain perspective, it is entirely real. The ego wants to continue existing, and if you wake up, what will happen then?

The ego desperately wants to keep experiencing, to keep colouring your light, to keep living. Oh, how it wants to persist in its perception of itself.

It will destroy love, destroy everything, even itself, to remain in the darkness of its dream, to keep the fluid in the glass the same. The labyrinth has no exit, no solution. You can't escape this trap by outwitting the labyrinth. Your own image of yourself, your image of others—who are, in fact, both your reflection and you walking a different path—create this labyrinth. It is infinite, and there is no exit.

At the ends of infinity, there's just another wall of this endless maze... You can't escape by looking for the one path, the one way out, because it doesn't exist. You have to see the obvious truth. Looking at the past is useless; you already know you haven't found the exit. You've checked. Looking ahead or to the sides is just as pointless... There is no exit from this labyrinth; it is infinite. You can't keep staring at your feet forever, because while you'll stumble less, suffer less, you'll also see less, learn less, and fail to understand the truth that you're still surrounded by walls built by your own dream, by yourself. You can't destroy them, just as you can't destroy yourself... you're still stuck in the labyrinth... After experiencing the vastness of reality, after walking countless paths in the labyrinth, there always comes a time to end the journey. The experience has been gathered, the lesson has been learned. You've done so much, and it's simply enough now. It's time to wake up... It's time to reach into your pocket and pull out the key that's always been there. There comes a time to realize the obvious and simple fact that the only real way out of the endless labyrinth is to look up, to leave the endless walls behind, and rise like a feather above them, above this dream, and regain the freedom that you've never really lost, but merely forgotten for a fleeting moment... You are a drop of water in the ocean.

There is only the ocean, yet you also exist, and nothing will ever change that."

"That was quite a monologue, but in that case, why do we need the dark ones? Wouldn't it be better to just destroy them all?"

"The so-called dark ones are beings who have forgotten and strayed farthest from their light. Their glass is the least transparent, filled with a murky liquid. In their concept, they serve God by exalting His presence in themselves while denying that God exists in others. They have developed their power for control and dominion because by diminishing others through comparison, they exalt their own spark. In truth, from the Creator God's perspective, they unconsciously perform a very necessary task. At the same time, they are incapable of harming who you truly are or what truly matters. In a wise dream, the dreamer may experience terrible things, but it can never actually harm the dreamer themselves, though it may gift them with great lessons and important experiences. Through their "evil" nature, the dark ones inspire good beings to grow so that by defending against evil, they advance on the path of knowledge, compassion, and love. Without evil, there would truly be no motivation, without challenges there would be stagnation. The experiment with the mouse utopia, where giving everything, in fact, takes everything away, is a great example of this. In truth, evil also serves God, but from a human perspective, it's difficult to grasp this properly. The ultimate goal of dark beings is also to awaken from their dream and realize the truth on their own path, but until that moment, they serve the good beings through the eternal dance of experience."

"So, why did God create all of this in the first place? What's the point of all this chaos? Wouldn't it be simpler if none of it existed?"

"What would love be without the possibility of expressing it? What would knowledge be without the chance to share it? What would wisdom be without manifesting it? Personally, I believe that loneliness was the mother of creation, and the father was the being who gave us everything."

There was a long silence. I literally didn't know what to say. Finally, I blurted out a question and immediately feared that I had asked too much.

"But what about the Dark Ones? What do you plan to do?"

"The dark side has grown too strong and has united. They are needed, but in excess, they can disturb too many paths, cause too much destruction. They are unaware of how much harm they can cause. They now possess enough power to dominate the entire galaxy. With or without pretence, they will strike, and if they succeed, it will bring aeons of suffering and downfall across the galaxy. Our last chance is to cut off the dragon's head before it spreads its wings and casts its shadow over everything. I'm now gathering my fleet, my personal guard, and we'll strike at the heart of darkness, at the place where their leaders meet. If we succeed, their forces will again splinter into warring factions, and the galaxy will be safe once more."

"Why are you telling me all of this? Shouldn't this be classified information I shouldn't know about?"

"In your Akashic record, we had this conversation. Now we are doing what was planned. What had to happen."

"What about me?"

"Don't worry. Tomorrow you'll return home and be with your loved ones."

"I don't know if I want to go back. This Earth is full of so many wonders I haven't yet discovered, there's still so much for me to explore. Can't I stay a little longer?"

"Everything has its time, and everything happens for a reason."

"General, the fleet formation is complete. All units are in position. We are ready for the jump." – A voice echoed through the hall where we stood.

"The people who answered my call and are now gathered around me, they're not just my subordinates. They're my family, my children and friends; they're the path we've been walking together for so long. It's time for us, but it's also time for you. It's been a pleasure talking with you, John of Burton, but it's time for you to return to your home, time to say goodbye."

Suddenly, without warning, I found myself next to my cab. Mindlessly, I got inside, and we started moving, passing through the wall back to Earth, which is either his daughter or his home. Maybe both at once? I thought about what he had said to me, wondering who he really was and why all of this had happened to me.

"They're all here, the entire Legion of Light responded to Lord Romasz's call. I've never seen so many of their ships in one place."

"Aru Ashente!" I heard Romasz's cry in my head.

"Aru Ashente!!" These words filled my mind.

"ARU ASHENTE!!!" Millions of voices from the entire legion spoke at once.

Suddenly, everything went quiet. The countless swarm of ships, led by the flagship, vanished as abruptly as if they had never been there. They had left for a battle that no one knew about, but they had taken it upon themselves because it was the only way to save the galaxy, even if its inhabitants were unaware.

Good does good not because someone is watching, but because it must.

"I've never heard it personally before." I heard the quiet voice of the assistant.

"What do those words mean?"

"I don't know, no one knows except for the Legion of Light, but they always say them when they go into battle, and this time, they all showed up."

We returned in silence. We didn't exchange a single word. Time seemed to stand still. Whatever those words meant, I felt deep inside that my spark, whatever it was, fully understood their meaning. It fully knew what they represented. That feeling, so elusive, yet so deep and all-encompassing, filled me with silence, which at the same time expressed so much.

On the way back, I didn't even notice the fleet orbiting Earth or the magnificent city we were approaching. None of it mattered anymore.

In some inexplicable way, those words, those words shouted by millions of voices, those words that expressed everything, burned into my soul like a living fire. "Aru Ashente," whatever that means. I know I will never forget it, nor the feeling that filled me when I heard it.

10 THE LAST EVENING

I woke up late, very late. It was well past lunch already. The fact that I had returned late at night, or rather, in the early hours of the morning, didn't surprise me, but I had slept a long and deep sleep.

Some part of me must have needed to process everything. In the end, I wasn't sure whether Romasz was just a man or something more, but the depth of his understanding surpassed anything I had ever encountered. It surpassed any philosophical system or belief I had ever come across, and yet it was so simple to understand. I once heard that you can tell if someone truly understands something if they can explain it easily. The more complex the explanation, the less the person really understands, using complicated words to hide their ignorance. My conversation with him was etched deep into my memory, and I would never forget it.

I ate something, but although the food was as delicious as always, it didn't taste as good any more. I felt an emptiness, as if I had lost something very important. I didn't know what to do with myself.

Perhaps that conversation had caused far more confusion in my value system than I had expected, and as a result, I felt this unspeakable loss. Perhaps, deep down, I sensed that I could have learned much more from him, but I knew he would never find the time to talk to me again.

It was probably a great stroke of luck that I even had the chance to speak with him at all.

Without thinking, I turned on the television to break the unbearable silence. Maybe mindlessly watching would help me relax and put all the pieces in their proper places.

On the screen, a reporter was shouting his words in terror.

"The Legion of Light, Lord Romasz's fleet, has been completely destroyed! No one survived! It was a trap! They jumped right into the centre of the enemy fleet! The Dark Ones had an overwhelming advantage! The Legion didn't stand a chance. Everyone perished, every single one. The galaxy has lost its defender. The Dark Ones have launched an attack along the entire frontier, mercilessly crushing any resistance. They used Lord Romasz's attack as a pretext to declare war. Countless worlds have fallen under the pressure of the enemy's terrifying superiority..."

The reporter spoke these words in a frantic voice.

"The Galactic Council is calling for peace talks, but so far, they haven't received any response. The Dark Ones' assault is spreading across the galaxy, and no one seems able to stop them."

I turned off the television. Everything was clear now. The Dark Ones would have attacked, pretext or not. This attack had been inevitable, but the council's short-sightedness had prevented them from seeing it. As usual, those in power made mistakes, and ordinary people paid the price. Some things never change.

Lord Romasz and his magnificent fleet were no more. I didn't know what would happen next. The power of his fleet had seemed nearly infinite, and yet they had fallen. Could a god truly die?

I asked Kaselin if I could visit Anatea. She didn't mind, not that I thought she cared much about anything right now. Her entire world view had crumbled, and nothing seemed to matter any more.

I used the pin and transported myself to the little girl. In some magical way, my fears no longer mattered. I could even die, and what difference would it make? Would anyone notice?

She stood sadly outside her house. It was already late at night, and everything was enveloped in an indescribable silence. It was as if the entire planet was mourning its father. As if the whole planet was plunged into grief.

"My dad hasn't spoken to me," Anatea said. "He always contacts me when he's on a mission, but this time, he didn't. He always does that. I don't understand why he couldn't talk to me this time." Tears rolled down her cheeks, and her body trembled with the shudders of despair.

I hugged her tightly, and in silence, I stared at the starry sky. Not a single cloud dared to obscure that magnificent sky. I had never seen so many stars in my life. In the city, you can only see a fraction of what you could here. It was as if something was trying to console the beings inhabiting Earth. The silence was dreadful, but also extraordinary at the same time.

As if the whole planet was singing a requiem expressed in an all-encompassing silence...

Meanwhile, in the far reaches of space on the outskirts of the solar system, a sudden swarm of immense, almost uncountable Dark One's warships appeared.

"Ship has arrived at the assembly point, Admiral."

"Finally, we will have our revenge on him and destroy everything he holds dear for preventing us from claiming our rightful place in the galaxy for aeons. But he paid the ultimate price for his arrogance, and now, everyone associated with him will pay that price as well. We will destroy everything he built. We will erase his name from the annals of history. We will make sure that all who remember him will join their god in the afterlife."

"All units are in position, Admiral. We're ready to strike."

"Good, move the entire fleet into high orbit around Earth. We're not going to play games with them. This will be a total annihilation. Destroy everything in our path, no mercy, no chance of survival. Complete destruction of Romasz's home. They will pay the ultimate price for their crimes against our race. Take no prisoners, let no one escape. There must be no witnesses, no records of what's about to happen. A devastating strike creates fear in our enemies, but total silence about how it was done will stir boundless terror. Raise the isolation barrier around this system. Nothing gets out, no signal penetrates. No one will interfere. There will be no witnesses.

There will be no songs or stories. Only the horror of absolute ignorance of how we achieved this."

"Admiral, the approach vector indicates a dangerously close pass near the seventh planet, called Jupiter by the locals. I suggest deactivating the passive shields and leaving only the force and reflective shields operational."

"A major battle is about to begin, and you suggest deactivating a significant portion of our fleet's defence systems?"

"Admiral, passive shields distort space-time, making it significantly harder to hit anything, but they generate a strong local gravitational distortion. Our synchronized graviton emitters compensate for this field at the level of combat units, but externally, our fleet creates a massive gravity well. This will result in gravitational capture by that planet, bringing it into a closer orbit of the system. The computer simulation predicts this will cause it to swap places with the planet called Saturn, leading to serious repercussions."

"I don't see the problem. Does this pose any threat to our fleet?"

"No, Admiral, but it will cause catastrophic, long-term gravitational disturbances throughout the entire local planetary system."

"At a time like this, you bother me with such insignificant matters? This is the moment of our great glory, our great victory. Generations have awaited this moment, and you're concerned with trivialities. I'm starting to doubt if you're the right person for this position."

"Yes, sir, I understand. I will do my utmost to fulfill my duties without distracting you with matters unworthy of your attention," The Chief Science Officer replied, his face showing deep fear. He had seen high-ranking officers lose their lives for far lesser "offences" under unexpected conditions on penal planets, where the only source of sustenance was other prisoners.

"Have the shields been raised as I ordered?"

"Yes, sir. The isolation barrier is functioning perfectly. No ship, no signal can penetrate it. Our technicians made no errors."

"You'd better be right, because just like the technicians, you too can be easily replaced by someone more competent."

"Yes, sir."

"But this means we have time, we can have some fun. Let's show our prey what we're capable of, what they'll face when we reach their position. Such terror should generate additional sustenance for which we'll surely be rewarded. Adjust course. On the way to Earth, we'll practice bombardment on the system's fifth planet."

"Intercept course set, Admiral."

"Excellent. Prepare the gravitational charges. We won't waste our main weapons. Let's also see how well we achieve the theoretical assumptions. There's nothing like practice, and practice makes perfect."

"We're within range, Admiral."

"What are you waiting for? Fire a volley and return to course toward our main target."

"Yes, sir. Orders issued."

"There's nothing like playing with prey before the final strike... What are these tremors? Who dares to attack us? There were no reports of a counterattack!"

"No enemy actions detected within effective range of standard weaponry."

"Then what's causing these tremors?"

"The fifth planet, as predicted by simulations, entered into harmonic seismic tremors, and the overlapping shock waves greatly amplified their amplitude, causing catastrophic fractures across the entire width of its outer mantle. Unfortunately, the predictions didn't account for such heavy bombardment of a relatively small planet, and it lost its integrity. It appears we'll need to make a small adjustment to the system's maps, as it simply couldn't withstand the assault and shattered into countless fragments. Fascinating sight."

"A rather unfortunate event, but of no real consequence."

"Would the Admiral like to know its name?"

"Why? It's no longer there. Who cares about insignificant objects? Our target is Earth."

"Sir, the soul of Earth is too strong, it carries the spark of Romasz. Its light will annihilate any of us who approach it. The planetary shield is also one of the best in the galaxy.

Long-range bombardment will be ineffective. We cannot win this battle."

"You doubt the power of the 167th Strike Fleet of our united empire? We are the best of the best, which is why the Emperor entrusted us with this mission. Arrest him; he will pay the ultimate price for his treason."

"That's how you deal with the ambitious before they gain support. I have a talent for eliminating threats before they become real problems," thought the Admiral with clear satisfaction and admiration for his own astuteness, so crucial in the position he held.

"Admiral, the group of ships stationed in orbit reports unconditional surrender."

"What kind of army surrenders before a battle?"

"These are civilian ships. Mostly ambassadorial, transport, and residential units. They hold no combat value."

"The worse for them. Only a true idiot would waste resources building ships without any combat capability. We'll use them for target practice. This will send an additional message to our enemies that we will not tolerate any weaknesses on their part.

"Sir, but they're surrendering. What about the rules of war? They don't belong to this star system; they are only here as guests."

"We are the law now. We define reality, we define everything. Our power knows no limits, and it knows no mercy. This will be a clear and final message: either the remaining races kneel before us, or they die. And if they find themselves in the wrong place at the wrong time, they will always face the same consequences: total annihilation at the hands of the Empire. I hope I am making myself clear, or do you wish to join your fellow tribesman for his disloyalty to our cause?"

"No, Sir. It won't happen again."

"No mercy! We take no prisoners! Open fire!!!"

The enormous fleet moved towards Earth, sweeping everything in its path. Any resistance was utterly futile. The enemy's advantage was far too great for anything to be done. Nothing even slowed the march of death as it moved toward destruction.

"The enemy forces have been completely annihilated. All units orbiting have been utterly destroyed with no losses on our side, Admiral."

"Excellent, everything is going perfectly, just perfectly. This is a total and glorious victory on the long path of our holy conquests. Now there's nothing left to do but execute the final stage of our plan. Issue the orders according to our original strategy. No adjustments are necessary. As always, we have anticipated every element, and no, even the smallest, adjustments are needed."

The entire operation had been planned long ago and carried out down to the smallest detail. We won't need to land on the planet. We'll simply bring our battle station closer, which has been added to our fleet, and its gravitational influence will draw huge amounts of water from the oceans. Thanks to Earth's rotation, they will create such an enormous tsunami that even the ocean floors will not remain intact. We will kill every human and destroy every trace of Romasz's work. We will wipe this civilization off the face of the Earth. Planet soul will not withstand the suffering of billions of beings and will sleep for long aeons, leaving the planet unprotected. Then we will choose some group from the surviving species and genetically develop them to a semblance of human beings. They will live short lives and in suffering, and their torment will generate the low energies that serve as our food. This will be the ultimate degradation and desecration of Romasz's creation. When other civilizations see what we have done, not knowing how we managed to achieve it, they will not have the courage to stand against us. No one will ever raise their head against us again, and our rule in this galaxy will be unchallenged forever.

"Execute the order. Initiate Omega Protocol, the final destruction of Earth, the ultimate destruction of the Great Galactic Genetic Library, the complete destruction of Romasz's work. We will kill and destroy everything he has touched, everything he has influenced, leaving nothing to mourn. No one will question our power, our superiority over all species. At last, we will take our rightful place."

At the same time...

I held her tightly, looking up at the stars. The silence around us was unbearable. Every living creature sensed that something terrible had happened, and something even more horrifying was coming. Everything that lived had hidden wherever it could, and I just stood there, holding her, not knowing what else I could do.

Suddenly, in the starry sky, I saw one point of light growing larger and larger. At first, I didn't know what was coming toward us, but as the object grew bigger, I finally recognized its familiar shape. It was our moon, our beloved moon, and somehow, I hadn't noticed its absence before. I hadn't paid attention.

But it kept getting bigger, closer and closer to the planet. I had never seen it so huge before. It kept growing, becoming larger and larger with every moment, until it filled one-third of the sky. A strong wind rose, and in the distance, I heard the far-off sound of rushing water. Everything was so unreal, terrifying, yet beautiful at the same time. The roar of the water grew louder with each passing moment, its noise building.

The moon stopped as if gazing down at Earth for the first time. As if they had never looked upon each other before. It and the Earth, in a terrifying dance. The deafening roar drew nearer, and the girl pressed herself closer into my arms. I could do nothing but hold her tighter.

Then I saw it. A colossal wave, as high as mountains, was rushing towards us with a terrifying, thunderous roar, sweeping away everything in its path. The moon gazed on dispassionately as the spectacle unfolded. Life disappeared in silent helplessness. Finally, it reached the spot where I stood...

EPILOGUE

Everyone was dead, and I was oddly certain of that. Deep inside, I felt an overwhelming sense of loss and grief, almost like mourning someone very important in my life.

Did Romasz know what was coming? Did he manage to keep his glass clean in the face of losing everyone he loved so deeply? Was that meeting with him meant to convey something deeper, to lead to something significant? Or was it merely a tribute, written into the Akashic Records? Had all of this really happened, or was it just a product of my wild imagination?

The stars, which had always looked the same, shining with their eternal glow. The Moon, the ancient wanderer, come from afar, whose fate had been sealed in such dramatic circumstances. Every night he watched over the Earth and its inhabitants. So many lovers had experienced beautiful moments in his light; so many songs and poems had been born because of him. Mysterious and silent, shrouded in secrecy.

During a full moon, every soul feels his influence—a mix of magic, mystery, fascination, and a strange unease that runs deep, as if standing at the threshold of a door of no return, behind which lies the ultimate secret of existence.

Are we subconsciously feel what he is, where he comes from, or if it's just a deeply buried, traumatic memory of a dormant Earth that somehow projects onto us when we see him in full glory. Ancient knowledge of what he did to us in times long forgotten, times that almost no one remembers anymore.

www.ingramcontent.com/pod-product-compliance
Lightning Source LLC
Chambersburg PA
CBHW020630130626
46552CB00003B/1153